Carry Me On

CATHLEEN ELLIS

YOUNG PEOPLE IN LOVE IN THE HEARTLAND OF AMERICA

OTHER BOOKS BY CATHLEEN ELLIS

www.CathleenEllis.com

A Scarf of Promise

Castle in the Air

Making Our Way

Kara's Love

Baskets on
Christmas Lane

Up To Me

Christmas Bright

A Voice for Gabby

Love Ties

Roses for Meredith

Old Crooked Road

Just Let It Go

Tend My Flowers

Together Now

Sky Tossed

Humble Task

What's Beneath

Loving Presence

Shadow to Sunshine

Future Bright Light

Compass North

Running Shadow

I'm Mortuary Girl

Back to Now

To The Beet

1

"Give what you have. To someone, it may be better than you dare to think."

Henry Wadsworth Longfellow

Fall – Sophomore year

Students talking and laughing rang through Bree's ears as she gazed around the sunny lunchroom. French fry smells tickled her nose. She spotted a bent over girl as she sat alone at one of the far tables. She walked across the lunchroom and stood next to the girl.

"Uh, c'n I join you?"

"Suit yourself," she heard the quiet voice.

Bree sat down next to her and put down her lunch sack and carton of milk. She held out her hand, "I'm Bree Newland, first year at your school."

Lori looked her in the eye as they shook hands, "Lori Grifson, sophomore, you?"

"Same, just gonna be here for a year, living with my grandmee, Betty Newland."

"Elementary school teacher?"

"Uh huh."

"Remember her name from elementary school I attended, but didn't have her as a teacher. I've lived in Ony Springs my whole life. Here for just a year?" she gave Bree a wide-eyed look.

"Yeah, my folks're missionaries. They're in Angola right now, for a family who wasn't able to complete their two-year missionary time. Stability for me, that's what my folks want."

Bree paused, and Lori saw her winsome smile and nod, "My grandmee'll provide that." She shook her head, "Didn't wanta ship out to Africa with them. I want high school, here, now, in the good old US of A."

Bree watched Lori's green eyes brighten with interest.

"What then?"

"My folks'll be posted somewhere in the United States, wherever their church sends them."

"So you'll finish up high school, go on to college?"

"Sure hope so," Bree nodded.

They ate in silence.

"Hey, I'll just ask," she thought.

"Lori, whatcha think about having lunch together, to get to know each other?"

Lori gazed at Bree, seeing her almost black eyes and shining ebony hair. For the first time Bree saw her smile.

Bree caught another smile and a nod.

"I'd like that. I go straight home from school every afternoon 'cept Wednesday and Thursday. I help my mom at the café where she's a waitress. Those two days she's on a 12-hour shift. I wait tables, bus, do dishes, close, but no cooking 'cause they got a great cook. I get a little spending money. And you know, there's never enough of that for stuff I want."

Bree nodded her head in agreement, "Never enough of that."

They smiled to each other.

Lori and Bree ate lunch together every day after their first meeting.

And before long Bree asked Lori to visit after school.

Lori gazed around as she came through the great room to the kitchen.

"Wow, Bree, your grandmee has such a lovely home. It's so clean, uncluttered. Oh, she loves pale violet, blues. How do you and grandmee accomplish all this; everything's so nice?"

Bree shared with Lori the secrets of grandmee's housekeeping success, while working as a teacher all her life.

"Place for everything, everything in its place." Bree giggled and shook her head, "Sometimes a little dusty,but not messy, that's the secret."

Lori marveled at Bree and her comments.

"This girl makes good sense,"Lori told herself as the two teens got to know each other.

A couple of weeks later Lori got up the courage to bring Bree to Christmas Lane. They walked home together after school one Tuesday afternoon. Lori's folks worked days, along with her older brother who helped manage a gas station.

Bree looked around Lori's dirty and cluttered kitchen. Papers and dishes littered the table. Lori washed two glasses from the pile of dirty dishes sitting on the counter. They shared a soda.

Lori smiled to Bree, "So great to be with you at your grandmee's. I've never really been in a nice home here in Ony Springs."

"Hey, from what you've seen, what'cha think?"

"So different."

"What about helping, more effort from you?"

"Yeah, I can do more."

"And just like you and me, we talked, you're taking an interest in your classes for the first time."

"Uh huh, my teachers've always told me that I'm super smart. I lack motivation." Lori looked at her friend, "I," she paused, "I'm starting to get that a little bit. You know what?"

"What?'

"You really encourage me to try; I'm changing."

"Yup, that's my family, way we are, giving what we have, helping folks to make better for themselves."

"Oh Bree, my family," she stopped talking, then shook her head, "is so tired after work. Sometimes we cook up eggs and toast. Then my folks crawl to bed. Dad and mom always tell me to go to school, to stay in school."

Bree watched her drooping eyes.

"That's all they ever say," Lori spoke in her quiet voice.

"You know how to cook?"

"Uh huh, I do, yeah, I could make simple dinners on Mondays, Tuesdays and Fridays, 'cause mom and I work until 7 p.m. on Wednesday and Thursdays, and then we each get a free meal at the café. We always bring some of that food home for my dad and brother."

"Hey, I'd like to try to help you. What about I give you a hand with kitchen clean up? And if you'd let me, I'd give your beautiful dark hair a trim." She nodded to Lori, "I cut hair for friends from past years."

"Bree, what about your homework and helping out your grandmee with her home?"

She smiled to Lori, "Will get that done when I get home. I can help you."

℘

They worked together making order, washing, drying and putting away dishes, sweeping and mopping the kitchen area. Lori sorted through the papers on the table and put them in a folder for her folks

Lori spoke up, "For sure you're wondering why I sat alone in the school lunchroom, on your first day at Ony Springs High."

"Please tell me."

"I'm quiet, plain, tall. Always had trouble making friends." Lori shook her head, "ashamed of my clothes, of our home."

Bree watched as Lori's face brightened to red.

"Never invited any girl over, no sleepovers for me, ever. Lots of poor folks, mostly renters, live here on Christmas Lane. In past years, long gone, a sawmill company built 20 homes on our street. They rented these small homes to workers in the sawmill. When the sawmill company left Ony Springs, well, the houses stayed. And you see what's happened. Landlords rent out. And some rental families do keep their houses up."

Lori sat down at a kitchen chair.

"My stupid pride," Lori shook her head, "always been a, a problem for me. But you helping me, just beginning to do simple things to make my life better."

They moved to the bathroom. Bree trimmed off four inches of Lori's hair. With the curling iron Lori seldom used, Bree showed her how to curl the ends of her hair.

"Unbelievable, Bree."

"Your hair, beautiful, several shades of auburn and brown together. You see that now?"

"I do," Lori nodded to Bree as they saw their smiles in the bathroom mirror.

"Light-hearted, and caring, that is what you are to me, Bree."

They hugged.

&

For several months Bree and Lori spent time together on Tuesdays. They often met at Lori's home on the far end of Christmas Lane.

They poured their sodas into glasses and sat at the kitchen table.

"Mom and dad, they own this home. They put in a new furnace and central air conditioning when they bought it. And they added a bedroom and bathroom to the back of the house. There's love here, uh, and they're super proud of this place.

But they struggle every day, to put food on the table. They'll go without to make sure my brother and me," she paused, "well, that we get enough to eat. No matter what," Lori nodded, "they'll make the mortgage payment."

"Home ownership means a lot to them."

"Oh, it's everything."

Lori stopped talking and thought of what she should say next.

"They come from families who rented farm places up in the hills of way north Georgia. All my grandparents passed on, hard times. And my dad's sister, and my mom's brother, almost no communication, ever."

She shook her head, "One home dad lived in growing up had dirt floors for years. He swore he'd have better for mom and us."

"The appearance around here, have your folks said anything to you?"

"'Thanks, darlin' is all dad said, once. But mom, she's told me a couple of times how nice things are. She apologizes 'cause she grew up with zero model of good housekeeping."

"Yeah, you know how to keep up, just a little each day."

They stood at the door to Lori's bedroom.

"Bree, my room, stuff I love I keep out, my trusty stuffed tiger, my few books I read over and over. I'm learning to put away what I don't need in the closet and drawers."

She smiled to her friend. Bree caught a sparkle in Lori's eyes, a bright look for her.

"You helped me clean up my mess, my room. Uh, hang stuff up, duh." They giggled together. "You and me, we found a bedspread for me at the Thrift Store. And unbelievable, my family now has pillowcases, for the first time for our pillows. I am proud," she smoothed her pillow, "I did a little thing, for my whole family."

Lori paused, "Hey, three outfits, at the thrift store, you helped me. It's nice stuff for me, no one wanted them. I can't believe anyone would give those clothes away. I like the way I'm starting to look, my whole appearance."

She smiled to Bree.

"I'm glad, oh," she paused and shook her head, "all these things I take for granted, Lori. I hope you don't think I'm too bold in helping out."

Lori came to Bree, and they hugged.

"I am grateful to know you, and I follow up on stuff you suggest to me. You are always so positive, smiling, and light-hearted."

"Dance?"

"Yeah, let's practice that dance step you showed me, Bree. I been dancin' around in my room, trying to remember. You move so smooth, glide along."

They stood in the living room, Lori keeping her eye on Bree as she danced a little ahead of Lori. Bree kept singing the song, the rhythm taking them in.

"Enough," Lori exclaimed. "Gotta save energy for the job."

"You're doin' good, girl, with the dance practice. You learn quick."

That afternoon they chatted as they tackled the mess of junk in the Grifson front yard. Trash service came by the next day. In Ony Springs all trash, no matter how big or small or how much, got picked up on Wednesdays. Bree asked about a couple of pieces of car parts.

"It all goes, including the bikes, beyond repair."

They took a break with sodas after clearing the front.

"I'm so glad I had old stuff you could wear, Bree. It's warm out here, dirty work, and you helped make it so much easier, wow, so much nicer. "They'll pick it all up."

"Uh huh, a clean look, and ya know, there's grass under this stuff?"

"Yeah, once my brother and me cleaned up, but not for a while."

After they raked the near dead grass and bagged it up, Lori found an old garden hose from the back. She set a sprinkler to water the front lawn.

"Front porch, clear it?" Bree called to Lori.

Lori gave her a thumb up. Bree hauled pots of dead flowers, a planter, and broken wood to the trash pile. She found a broom and swept the concrete front porch clean.

The teens stood on the sidewalk and high fived each other.

"Unbelievable, Bree, wow, so nice. What about the back?"

Looking around the back yard they decided to work on it the next Tuesday.

"Girl, ya know what comes next?"

"Ick, grumble, grumble, leaves."

Lori smiled to Bree.

"Easier clean up."

"Gotta go."

"Hey, before you do, lemee show you our garage, my dad's big pride."

Lori unlocked the side door and turned on the bright light. Bree walked all around the inside of the garage. Oil, grease and gasoline smells tickled her nose.

"Wow, your dad, this place is so neat, all swept up."

"Dad's, uh, real proud of his tools, accumulated over many years. He and Nils work on cars in here, on Saturdays."

"Right, with your family's expertise, you guys won't worry about cars being in trouble."

Lori smiled to her, nodding, "Thank you for everything, Bree, for the changes you've help me make."

"How's the schoolwork?"

Bree watched her nod.

"Yeah, I got more energy to do my work. Grades improving, and I've gotten a couple of compliments, for trying. I carve out time at night, study on my floor, with my books around me. Oh, and quiet music, I listen to the old songs."

"I'm proud of you, Lori."

They hugged. Bree saw the tears in Lori's eyes, happy tears.

ૐ

"What's happened here?"

Lori heard his harsh voice, grinding out the words.

"Go away, don't want to see you," Lori shook her head to him, "ever again."

He glared at Lori as she stood at her front door.

"Dad, please come to the front door," she spoke out in a loud voice.

Lori's dad appeared.

"You understand? Please, don't come back."

He heard the firm tone. Jared backed away from the big man. He turned and walked down to his old sedan.

"She looks really good, something about her hair, her eyes, and this place," he spoke out. "Looks nice, they've done a lot of clean up around here."

"Another guy?" his mind drifted as he sped away, "time for another girl for me. This one's way young."

"Oh my gosh, Dad, thank you for helping me. He's a guy I won't spend time with, what the heck was I thinkin'?"

She shook her head as she gazed up at her tall father.

Lars Grifson grinned to Lori. "Happy to hear you say that, few months ago I worried about you seeing him, mostly at the café. He's a dropout. I want so much for you to finish high school, go on for training, or even college."

"Dad, it's what I think about, too. Can begin to imagine, well, my friend, Bree, she encourages me, helping me to change, making me stronger in my resolve. I'm beginning to understand what might be possible in my life."

"I gotta meet Bree; your mom wants to. Why not invite her to go to church with us and have lunch with us after?"

"Got it, Dad," she nodded, smiling to him.

Lori called Bree, asked her to come for church and Sunday lunch.

"Oh Lori, thanks, I want to meet your folks."

"And Bree, you know that nasty guy who bugged me at the café?"

"Yeah, what happened?"

"He stopped by, hated the way he talked to me. Dad helped me get rid of him. I want respect. I look around in my classes and I see decent guys."

"Give yourself time, Lori. Guys do notice you. I pay attention in our Spanish class. One day you will date."

"Same for you, Bree."

℁

Several Sundays later the Grifson's drove home from church with Bree and Lori.

"You have a jubilant choir; I dig their spirit," Bree spoke out as they neared Christmas Lane.

She heard the parents laugh. Lori's mom added, "One of the best things about our small community church, the Lord does hear us, while we're together."

Bree shared about the much quieter choir and congregation singing at the church where she and her grandmee worshiped.

"The Lord's word and our speaking to Him, we church members converse in all different ways."

Murmurs of agreement passed among them.

Bree saw the pride her parents had for Lori, in the looks and statements she heard directed to their daughter. She smelled the tantalizing chicken as they sat down to eat. The four of them ate piece after piece of fried chicken, the corn, rolls, and salad completing the meal.

"Delicious, Nancy, may I have your recipe for the fried chicken? I wanta fix it your way for grandmee and me."

"Happy to write that down for you."

"Bree," Lars gazed at her, "we want to thank you for being Lori's friend and helping at our Grifson home."

"You're very welcome."

Bree shared a couple of assignments her parents participated in as missionaries.

"My favorite location, Detroit. My folks served two different churches there, over the years. It's what I love to do, assist folks, it's my parents' work for all their adult lives. Helping just passed on down to me, giving what we have."

"Want to show you ladies something as soon as we're done."

Lars stood, assisting with dish drying while Lori washed. Bree helped Nancy fix a mound of food for Lori's brother.

"Nils, he'll like this yummy meal we had. He's pullin' long shifts at the station," she nodded to Bree.

The teens followed Lars into a detached one-car garage. Bree took in the odors of oil and gas as she gazed around at the silver surface of the car.

"Almost done with this sweet set of wheels," he spoke out after he turned on the light. "I been workin' on it for a bit. Folks do hobbies." He smiled to Bree,

"This is mine, cars."

"Whatcha gonna do with it?"

Lars nodded, "Go ahead, the plan."

"At our church," Lori paused, "we got folks who don't have much, our family, whew, so much compared to some," she shook her head as she looked to her dad and over to Bree.

"The past three years, a big need for cars, to get church members to their jobs, and for lots of other reasons."

Bree noted the serious look on Lori's face and in the tone of her soft voice.

"People in our church, seems like bad stuff, unfortunate life actions keep happening to them. A church committee, if they see the need, locates a vehicle. Dad fixes it up. The committee gives the car to a church member who has a need."

Bree smiled as she gazed at Lori's dad and then at Lori, "Oh my gosh, wonderful, to help someone with that need. Sir, you have a gift, a God-given gift," she nodded

She watched his smile.

"I do; I believe my hands do His work. Before we go," Lars looked at his daughter.

"Lori, you need to know, my next project is for you. You need wheels. I realize you haven't asked for one."

Lori began to cry as he continued.

"You been savin' money for a long time. I hate that you have to ride your bike so far to help mom out at her Wednesday and Thursday shifts."

He shook his head and grimaced, "The weather, sometimes not so great."

Lars touched his daughter's shoulder, "Any money you make going forward, please put it aside for future schooling, whatever you decide. Your grades, you are doing so well, mom and I," he paused, "proud," he nodded to her.

"Oh Bree, can you believe it?" Lori questioned her.

"Yes, I can."

Lori and Bree hugged, then held on as they jumped up and down. Both Bree and Lori cried.

"Happy tears," they shouted out.

Nancy drove Bree and Lori back to grandmee's.

"Thank you for sharing your church service and Sunday meal with me. And I want to try your fried chicken recipe you wrote out for me."

As she got out of the car she heard Nancy, "Our pleasure, Bree."

ℬ

Holidays, a new century, 2000, and then spring arrived for Lori.

"Did ya do it?" Bree asked as she sat down.

Lori faced her across the table in the warm and noisy lunchroom.

"I did," she nodded, smiling. "It feels so good, my first real interview. Mrs. Langdon gave me the job, on the spot after I explained my waitress work. I told her I'd work very hard, the trail completion, my top priority. I ended it with my pledge that we'd get the trail done this summer. Rain, muckin' up the trail, might force us to do signage work on that kind of day."

"Sorry I won't be here to help with the trail, to see the completion. We'll call and write, so I'll know how you are, how the trail's progressing."

Bree gave her friend a high five. They hurried through their lunches. On the way to class Lori turned to her friend.

"You gave me so much of your time and energy, Bree. I am a changed person. May not get a chance to tell you, I am very grateful."

"I loved helping you," she nodded to Lori. "My folks, me, it's what we do, watch over others. Our Lord needs helpers; we're some of His helpers."

ℬ

The school counselor gave eye contact to each one of the group in the counselor's conference room.

"You're the Ony Springs High students the mayor picked for the summer grant project. Other workers are from a conservancy of community college students. Here's our mayor, Mrs. Langdon."

"Hello."

Lori watched the mayor's wide smile.

"So, I've given my spiel to another group. Uh, I'll do better with you, more organized," she nodded. "You relax, and I'll do the same."

Lori breathed in, sensing the tension lessening in herself and among the group.

"With your help we're creating a trail, from Pippin Corner up to Log Landing."

She passed out a map to each participant. Lori looked it over and pointed out marker signs and comments.

"More tourism in our area of Georgia, that's our goal. The wineries exist, are open and getting busier. So folks visit them. But we need an opportunity for families, something for little kids, and even for teens like you all, a place for the whole family, to walk together. It's RES, called recreation opportunity spectrum, getting folks outside, walking trails, more diversity. It amounts to the pleasures of being outdoors."

Lori sat up straighter.

Her mind stream went like this, "Wow, fun, being outside, uh, the heat, the bugs." She nodded.

Mrs. Langdon went on, "Timber cutting, long time ago, an industry over our north area. A narrow-gauge steam locomotive and cars went from near Pippin Corner, where the train travels now. This special train backed up at a gentle grade the two miles up to Log Landing. Back it came down with timber for transport by rail. That was in the early days. In later times trucks transported some timber to sawmills that once existed outside Ony Springs."

A hand shot up.

"Yes," she acknowledged the student.

"The railroad tracks?"

"Over the years, they got removed." The mayor shook her head, "Parts of track, stolen."

"Musta' really wanted the iron rails."

"Correct," she nodded to the group, "after World War II, a shortage of everything. So, railroad ties also disappeared. Except some got buried under debris in the forest."

Students spent the next few minutes looking over the map.

"The timeline?"

"Uh, that's the big question, but please put down June 5 to August 4. That is the time the grant allows.

"What about our rainy Georgia days?"

"Contingencies when we're mudded up."

Lori whispered, then smiled, "I thought of that, also."

"You'll be working, Monday through Friday, 7 a.m. to 3 p.m. Lunch is a half hour. The young person in charge of the trail making worked out the daily routine. Georgia's Department of Natural Resources guided him. Many times he's used his mileage device while walking the trail."

The mayor acknowledged another hand going up.

"So we'll know each day, the equipment we'll need, what the day's goal will be."

"Right."

"Wow," a student spoke out, "I can't believe I'll be getting paid for being outside, enjoying our Georgia beauty."

Lori heard clapping; she joined in, agreeing with him.

Mrs. Langdon waved to them.

"You'll need to remember spray, for all our buggies, sun screen, proper boots, gloves, rain gear, jeans and long sleeves. Lunch and lots of water, critical for you in your backpacks."

"It's gonna be so hot," a student spoke out with such emphasis the whole group laughed.

"'Course," she nodded.

છ

Lori sat with Bree and her grandmee, Betty Newland, at the dining room table. She gazed around the pale blue room with windows showing the flowers and green back yard. She looked to her friend.

"I'm sad, an ache right here," she touched her heart, "a missing you." Lori began to cry, "Oh Bree, you haven't even left."

Bree heard the sobs and touched Lori's hand.

"Same for me, I'm sad too, missing you."

Bree paused and gave her friend a big smile.

"You'll meet new people, Lori, especially this summer. It's always been easier for me, from moving often to a new missionary assignment."

"Where're you headed next?"

Betty and Bree smiled to Lori, "The USA!"

Lori clapped her hands.

"Two years left, maybe finish high school, uh, in one place?"

Bree nodded to Lori, "So that's what mom and dad say."

"Where?"

"A mostly Hispanic community, close to an Indian reservation in southeastern New Mexico."

"Well, how's your Spanish?"

"Now you're being a tease, Lori, we're in Spanish II together. My accent's passable."

"Girl, you're the best student in class, your speaking and grammatical expertise. Our teacher always tells us."

"Yeah, right."

"No, duh, you are, I'm paying you a compliment."

Lori gave her friend the evil eye.

Bree touched her hand and nodded. They finished the meal and took their plates to the kitchen. After cleaning up they fixed dishes of berries and ice cream for the three of them and returned to the table.

"I'll give you time together after we finish dessert. Bree, your packing's coming along?"

She smiled and nodded to her grandmee.

The teens sat next to each other, on the floor in Bree's light-filled peach room. They rested their backs against the bed.

"When will you be here again?"

Bree gazed ahead for a moment and then turned to Lori.

"Christmas holidays, I hope, Grandmee's invited my folks and me to visit. I'll have so many changes, again, in my life. I'm up for all possibilities, Lori."

"Maybe the week after Christmas?"

"Yeah, that's probably when."

"So wonderful," Lori's eyes shone into Bree's.

"Oh, I'll be right back," Lori jumped up.

She found her backpack where she put it earlier. Lori knelt beside Bree and handed her the white tissue-wrapped gift.

"Oh, it's so lovely, beautiful calligraphy. Lori, you did this."

"Yup, I took a class one summer at the community center. And I continue to work on my skills. I've had several commissions. Don't like painting, but I adore calligraphy."

Bree touched the bookmark, reading aloud, "Give what you have. To someone, it may be better than you dare to think. Henry Wadsworth Longfellow."

"It's so much, so much," Lori paused, "you."

"Oh gosh," she turned to Lori. Tears glazed her dark eyes as Lori watched her. "Not sure I've heard this quote before. Thank you. Will cherish the bookmark and keep it in the book I'm reading. I'll remember you, your special gift."

"From," Lori looked up, "above."

They hugged. Lori turned and got up on her knee. After she raised up she gave Bree a hand so she could stand.

"Bree, wish we could e-mail. No computer at home, so written notes and phone calls to each other, until next school year."

"Fine for me."

Their goodbyes came as her grandmee and Lori's mom walked ahead of them to Nancy's car. They turned to each other.

"Carry me on, in your thoughts, in your memories," Lori smiled to Bree.

"As I'll carry you on, Lori, I'll never forget how you responded to my suggestions, and how grateful you were as life got better for you. You bring me joy."

Lori waved and gave Bree and grandmee a tearful little smile as they drove away. Lori's chest burned as the car got to the street's end.

"It's gonna burst, my heart," she spoke out. Tears cascaded down her cheeks and onto her shirt. Nancy touched her daughter's shoulder.

"I'll never forget her, how she helped me to change into the person I am now. Oh mom, I love her."

Once they got out of the car at home Nancy came and hugged her daughter. She stepped back from Lori.

"And I love you, Lori," she spoke out as she smiled at her.

"Love you, Mom."

Falling on her knees that night Lori prayed, "Gotta make each day precious, special, must move on with my life. You are my refuge, my strength."

ℭℴ

Jedediah handed out hard hats to his trail workers. He explained completing a second year at community college and being a junior in the fall at the U. of GA.

"I'll study in the natural resources program. Doing this summer work, great for what I want in my future."

He pointed to the front of his hard hat.

"Tape, on mine, and on your hard hats.

"Yeah, I know it's hot out here, but the hard hat is mandatory. Plus I'll get to know you faster with your name front and center.

We work in many trees. Tremendous growth occurred in the years after the railroad abandoned the route. I will shoot photos as we go, showing improvements."

He smiled to them, breaking his serious tone, "It'll be an incredible difference."

Jedediah paused, "LAC, it's a term I use, and I want you to understand. It's Limits of Acceptable Change. As we build the trail we must keep in mind that we're not making big changes from what the constructors of the railroad tracks did all those years ago. We'll do our best to keep the forest look of the area on either side of the trail."

"What about trail erosion, after lots of folks walk the trail?"

"Right," Jedediah looked at his name tape, "Gavin, that's the other piece of LAC. We must find native materials right at the trail for surfacing, material that won't erode. An example: we take up several inches of trail, backfill with what's close and return the surface, will get the hang of it as we go. Remember, the goal is renewing the railroad trail."

He walked back and forth in front of the group and nodded his head.

"So my frustration level, horrible, the first few times I hiked this track. Often I stumbled and hacked my way through the growth. I knew the track had to be ahead and sloping up, I just," he shook his head and threw up his hands, "not there."

"Could get lost," Raymond spoke up.

"Exactly, gotta watch out for each other. Stepping away from the trail, yeah, possible. So we all gotta look to the right, the left, up, down, kinda our heads in motion as we go."

A worked called out, "Jedediah, an old name."

"Uh huh, not sure what my folks were thinkin'," he rolled his eyes a couple times. It got the group laughing.

"Please call me JJ, OK?"

"OK, JJ," they spoke in unison.

JJ reminded them of the safety involved in this trail construction. He asked for the liability waivers parents signed. One student had no waiver.

"I cannot allow you to stay."

The student walked away.

"And please do not return until the waiver is signed. And I'll need your hard hat."

The student stepped back to JJ and handed him his hard hat.

Lori watched him saunter off.

"Man oh man," she thought, "first impression, no way I'd work with him, ick."

For several minutes JJ identified each worker, with the liability waiver he or she turned in.

"I'm satisfied, ready?"

He heard a loud shout back, "Ready."

Three guys and two girls made up each of the teams. Lori looked around her, slim, in good shape, all of them.   The workers introduced themselves, the grade and the school they were from.

She stood straight and tall as she gave eye contact to each member of her group. Lori smiled the brightest smile she could muster.

"The youngest, only high school junior," Gavin thought, "Sophia and Lori go to my high school. Whew, I don't ever remember seeing Lori before."

Other team members attended community college and one belonged to a conservation corps. The corp sent him to the trail group for the summer.

"Sweet," Lori smiled to herself, "realize now why I carried big trays of food in the café, all the walking, refilling coffee and drinks, and oh my gosh, bussing. Prep work for this."

Trail work began. Everywhere low hanging trees and tall undergrowth impeded their efforts. Heat blasted their bodies and bugs bothered their faces. They stopped for lunch, backpacks not far away.

"I'm whining, we for sure didn't get very far."

Lori saw heads nod at the discouraging tone of one worker's voice.

"Slow, arduous work, not for the faint-hearted," JJ commented, smiling to the workers circling around him.

"Hey, why begin the trail here? It's aways from the area you said would be parking."

"Good question, this trail will not allow dogs or mountain bikes. Trailhead's a little hidden. That's to discourage just anybody from heading up the trail."

"That's where we'll put signage for the trail, more within the foliage?"

"Right, we're interested in hikers, in families out for a few hours. Back to work, half hour's up, enough water everybody?"

JJ saw weary heads nodding.

"We've cleared enough area. Let's talk about it, gather around."

JJ took his measuring device and laid it across the area to be trail.

"Couple numbers you'll use, 18" to 28", that's tread width. Other number, 12", width on either side of the trail.

"Uh, according to my math, it's a width of up to 52."

"Yes, Tami, about 4 ½ feet. Not that wide, but in places we will struggle, with the undergrowth and hanging tree limbs."

They group stood on either side of the trail. They agreed only one person could walk the trail at a time.

"Yeah, a narrow trail, for now, with more usage, possible we'll widen it," JJ spoke up.

"By 1:30 Lori's legs and her arms blazed like a hammer beating on them. Wiping above her eyes kept the constant sweat from pouring into her eyes. With the water break came an ache in her back.

Gavin noticed her bright smile, confidence, helpfulness, and her ease in handling the physical labor, and most of all her gleaming green eyes. He sensed she had hard work at some other job, to be as fit as she was. Two other group members struggled to walk.

JJ stopped work an hour later.

"Good news for all of us," he looked around at the group. "If we keep up the effort of today," he nodded, "we'll complete the project by early August."

"Uh," Cliff spoke up, "seemed like we didn't make much progress."

Lori watched as JJ stood back from them, keeping up his smile.

"We'll get used to this, a little bit at a time. On rainy days we'll meet at a workshop in the community center in Ony Springs. Signage work, making trail markers, we'll do that there. Tomorrow Spring County Roads will assist the city road's crew with a parking area for eight vehicles. We won't be alone."

Lori dragged her aching body to her locked-up bike.

"I guess I said goodbye to my group and JJ, don't really remember."

She pedaled home, showered and took a pain pill.

"I like Gavin, and the two guys in our group, but the girl, she'll never survive."

She lay on top of her bed, sunlight warming her, "Tomorrow?"

2

His group circled around him the next morning.

"Eight, we're down to eight. Didn't take long for workers to realize what the job entailed. Both my and Gavin's group lost a member, three guys and one girl in each."

He nodded to his remaining workers.

"More manageable, we won't get so much in each other's way. But we had to give the others a chance, right?"

"Right, JJ," Raymond spoke up.

"Let's see the parking lot area before we start."

Lori watched the county workers, with grading equipment and shovels. Logs stacked along one side of the area. Each log might indicate the front space for a parked car.

"I see eight logs, eight parking spots?" Lori asked.

JJ nodded to her and the group, "The conservancy wants only that many places. The time may come where they'll expand, but not now. Remember LAC, we don't want hikers to grow to large numbers."

"Destroying the trail, oh my gosh, that might happen," Trey spoke up.

"Exactly, we're building a small footprint now, for the future, not a super highway of hiking."

"Other hikers, where'll they park? I looked up and down this road, doesn't appear to be enough room on the sides of the road?"

"That's right, Sophia, not enough room. Serious hikers gotta park further back where there's more room on the sides of the road to park."

"So it depends on the hiker. If they wanta do the trail, they gotta do the walk."

JJ smiled, nodding to Sam.

&

By the third hour JJ began to hear the workers groan as their muscles protested. Lori enjoyed the work. She looked back and saw the difference, a real trail. She thought about her decision the first morning of summer work.

"Each afternoon I'll shower when I get home. Then rest, work on summer projects and my home chores," she announced.

If it hadn't rained for awhile she watered grass. She mowed both front and back yards to keep up the neat appearance. Bree suggested a tiny garden.

"Name a rose after me," she told Lori before she left.

The day after Bree went to New Mexico Lori planted pumpkin seeds in soil she turned over. She added plant food. Within a week she planted two small rose bushes.

"A garden, Bree, I have a garden," Lori shouted out as she finished the planting.

She placed her garden in a corner of the backyard, where she planned to watch the growing process every day from the kitchen.

"I love roses, and always wanted pumpkins, so this is for me," she shared with her parents when they asked.

Once again her mom and dad expressed their appreciation for her interest in caring for the home and yard.

To begin her final project she visited the city library. She picked books her junior English teacher suggested she read during the summer, to prep for junior year. From the list Lori picked books to be discussed in class during the year.

While fixing dinner she read the small Ony Springs newspaper produced every day of the week. Since Bree and she discussed community issues she became interested in reading the paper. She remembered her hot face, her embarrassment when Bree talked of situations in Ony Springs. Lori knew nothing about what went on in her town.

∞

Lori experienced confidence in her body and in her ability.

"I've never known before, oh Mom, my arms, my legs, I'm stronger every day. But you know what?"

"What's that?" her mom eyed her.

They stood together in the kitchen preparing the dinner salad.

"My café time, huge in helping get me in shape for trail work."

She hugged her mom's shoulder.

That night she pulled out her ink and pens from the desk drawer where she kept her project. She folded the white notecard in half. On the outside, using her favorite flowing calligraphy she wrote out a Shakespeare quote about being true to yourself. Inside she penned:

Bree,

Enjoy working outside, perfect job for me. Thank you for letting me know about the trail work. If you were still here, I bet you might be doing trail work, too.   Two groups of four work the trail.   Wow, I like my group leader, Gavin. Handsome, smart, plans on college, a senior at OSH. Starting to think about my future possibilities. Hey, you saw that in me when we first met.   Yes, best friend, right again, decent boys are out there. I work right along side of them. So, how's it going in NM?

Love, Lori

∞

Surprise awaited the work crews on Day Two of the second week of work. They removed debris and cut away tree branches the first hour. Ahead they observed a clearing. The two trail groups clapped, cheered out, and high-fived each other.

"Wow, I see where the railroad tracks were, those years ago," Lori peered ahead.

She squatted down and put her right hand on the ground to feel the gravel. In some places that gravel remained near the surface.   In her memory she recalled railroad tracks she observed in the past.   That day the workers made rapid progress, through the clearing and then up a slight incline.

Lori saw the upcoming wall of the forest and vegetation. She lowered her head as a depressing thought hit her.

"So far to go."

JJ pointed out an orange tie he placed on an upper tree branch.

"I placed that marker, and many like it on an earlier trip."

They stood around him.

"How many times've you been up this trail?"

"I think 25 times to get my bearings, figure out the mileage."

He gazed around at his group, "Hey, nature, I love being out in it. Fun, not work for me."

Several workers gave him raised eyebrows.

"For real, it's the second week, any complaints from me?

"Not once," someone spoke out.

"Uh, as good a time as any, my second week pep talk. Begin with a DREAM. DIVIDE problems, work them out, one by one. MULTIPLY the possibilities. SUBTRACT negatives to get started. ADD enthusiasm. GET to your GOAL."

He gave eye contact to several in the group.

"Goal?"

"Finish this trail," they shouted.

JJ gave a big thumb up. He heard clapping and cheering. Lori stayed happy all the rest of that day.

"We Will create this trail, I know it," Lori nodded.

ℇ

Lori watched the gray clouds on Wednesday of Week Two. The cooling wind kept everyone content as they worked through the underbrush. Mid-morning JJ called for a work break. The groups assembled.

"Where's Trey, uh, my right hand man?"

"Told me he needed the potty. I headed back here."

"OK, Sophia, everyone, look up, down, ahead, back, get your bearings, stay here. Let me head out alone. Remember, we talked about losing a worker, this thick growth."

Lori heard a faint scream, a few seconds after JJ moved ahead.

"The scream's from the left, ahead a little," she whispered to the group.

They heard the scream, louder and louder.

"Help me, help me," and more screams.

Silence held in the forest.

"It's Trey, in trouble," Sam shouted.

JJ returned, mashing and smashing reverberated from the trees and underbrush.

"Gotta locate Trey."

JJ's eyes dotted from worked to worker.

"Lori, Raymond, stay here, in case Trey makes his way back. The rest, follow me in the direction of the scream."

Lori's mouth dried up and her eyes teared, just thinking about what happened to Trey. She walked up and down the new trail.

"First aid, right Raymond?"

"Got it, we'll need to help him, once he's located."

Soon Lori heard no sound coming from the left area. Her tummy cramped, told Raymond and headed into the woods to potty. Sweat streamed down her face. She upchucked the water from earlier. Lori sat on a rock, waiting for her head to clear. She heaved herself up and walked slow back to where Raymond stood.

"You OK?"

"Nope, so scared for Trey. I puked, better now," she nodded to him.

"It's been awhile," Lori found herself on her knees, "I'm scared, God, help Trey, help the workers looking for him. Please keep them safe in Your loving arms."

Soon Lori saw Sophia hack her way through the growth on the upper left side of the just completed trail. JJ and Sam supported a groaning Trey as the rest of the workers emerged.

"We traded off, with the others; Trey's big, we're struggling."

They laid Trey down. Raymond assessed his body.

"What happened?"

"Mumbling about a fawn, and the baby's mother," Sam muttered.

"Trey's got a big contusion on the side of his head. Whew, good you slowed down the bleeding, good job."

He nodded to Trey and Sam.

JJ added, "He's got a monster bruise, right side of his ribcage. Bet he's got broken ribs, 'cause he's in agony, each time we take a step."

"A mother deer protects her young. Maybe Trey got crosswise with the mother and baby."

Raymond looked up and around at the distraught faces, "Yeah, blows from a deer."

"From hooves."

The guys took turns helping Trey back to the start of the trailhead. The worker who went back first had JJ's phone to call for help. He carried Trey's backpack plus his own and several tools. Sophia and Lori hauled down the remaining tools.

Lori heard Trey's cries and moans, then silence. As they headed down the trail Sophia murmured, "If he could pass out, a relief."

Lori and Sophia arrived at the trailhead to watch the EMT's lift Trey on a gurney, ready for transport.

"Never heard an ambulance wail this close," Lori watched as it sped away.

"God bless and keep Trey; that siren's paralyzing."

Workers found their way to JJ.

He nodded, "You're excused for the rest of the day. You will be paid for all your hours; I appreciate your help with Trey."

JJ gazed around, "Cliff will come with me in my car. Once the hospital let's us know I'll call each of you with Trey's condition. You are all worried."

He gave eye contact to each stone-faced worker.

ଇଚ

Lori rode her bike home at top speed after the early release from trail work. She paced around her home, unable to calm down. She showered and tried to read.

"Dear Lord, can't concentrate," she looked into the backyard. Heat and humidity blasted her as she watered the roses and pumpkin patch. She mowed the front and back yards.

"Wow, our yard, unbelievable, how nice, Bree you should be here to see this."

She raked up the grass and bagged it for the trash man. Sweat streamed down her back and face. She gave up trying to mop her face. After she started dinner, she hopped back in the shower, still unable to concentrate on anything but Trey.

"Concussion, two broke ribs, we've lost him for trail work. And the mother deer did strike him."

Lori heard JJ's softer voice on the phone.

"He wanted to be a part of this project, JJ, he's gotta be bummed."

"Sheez, he needed to work this summer, to save for college."

"Thanks for letting me know; think we'll finish the trail?"

"Uh huh, we'll stay on track. The group we got left, all seven are hard drivers."

"Trey, in the hospital?"

"Just overnight; his folks are with him."

"I'm praying for him."

"We all are, Lori, good night."

Lori smacked her right hand into her left palm, time after time.

ଇଚ

JJ moved his eyes from one worker to the next. They stood around him the next morning.

"Gorgeous eyes, gleaming, as they always are," he gazed at Lori.

He heaved a big breath, a sigh of relief the whole group heard.

"Calmer today, right?"

"Right," the group answered in unison.

"The rain forecast for later today?"

"We'll beat it," Sam spoke with emphasis, getting them all to laugh.

℘

The group watched the transformation as the cluttered mess became a trail.

"First mile, complete," JJ clapped, "after four weeks."

He cheered for his workers as they ate lunch together.

Claps and shouts resounded from the group.

"Gavin, he will share what's happening as we start the second mile, the second four weeks."

They turned their attention to Gavin.

"Back history, for you all, my mom, Rachel," he stopped, tearing up, "a wonderful mom," he nodded.

"She possessed a special skill, learned from her dad, growin' up in the mountains of north Georgia. Woodcarver, that's what she loved to do in her spare time, carve into wood to create beauty. It's just me in my family. Mom loved fairies, the whole world of make-believe little people.

She had a vision. She started with a crude map of a garden, where fairies and their friends could hang out. Mom carved characters to put in different locations in the garden.

Once she created the 8" characters she painted their faces and hair, then their outfits. Seven characters, fairies with wings, a gnome, a troll, and a wizard. She loved the project and planned to locate the fairy garden in our back yard."

Lori listened to Gavin, to his deep voice. She watched the animated way he told about his mom and the fairy project. He shook his head and she saw his eyes go downcast.

He paused for a few seconds and looked up to the group. He spoke in a halting voice.

"She never got to see her fairy garden. Dad and I lost her four years ago, when I turned 13."

"Oh Gavin, we are so sorry," JJ spoke up, "wanta share?

"Cerebral hemorrhage, she never woke up in the hospital. After the docs declared her brain dead."

Lori saw his tears start.

"Dad and I let her go home to the Lord."

"Losing those you love," Lori shook her head at the thought, "I can't fathom what that must have been like for Gavin and his dad."

JJ explained how he heard about the project Rachel created as Gavin grew into a teenager. JJ took that information to the trail-making committee.

"They snapped up the idea of incorporating a fairy garden."

JJ nodded to his group, "A little walking trip off the trail."

"Wow, for the little children," Sam spoke out.

"And for us big kids too," Sophia added as everyone laughed.

℘

JJ pulled Lori aside near the end of the Monday workday. Week Five of the project continued.

"You and Gavin talked?"

"Right, I got my instructions. I meet him tomorrow in the community center workroom."

She shook her head, "Uh, sorta guilty, shouldn't I be working the trail?

He looked into her luminous green eyes and shook his head, "We need your beautiful calligraphy for the signage. You have a gift, gotta take advantage of it."

She nodded, "Will do my best to complete the calligraphy quick as I can."

"That'll be good 'cause we're gonna create the fairy garden to the left side of the trail, in a small clearing. Oh, and the trail will be completed aways ahead."

He saw a note of concern in her eyes.

"So, the garden for little children, it needs to be at the first mile marker?"

"Exactly, little ones, they might get discouraged if they must walk too far to see the garden."

He paused, "Oh, the community center staff can come to you in the workroom. Yeah, that's if I need to talk to you, about your progress."

"I'll see you and crew," Lori paused and smiled to him, "when I see you."

JJ let out a deep breath as he stepped away.

"I could drown in the green pools of her eyes," he shook his head as he walked away. Another thought hit him, "I'm not the only one attracted to Lori, Gavin, he sees what I see."

❧

Lori walked into the workroom at the community center. She smiled, looking around, and seeing windows.

She moved close to the windows, "Oh, good, they're open so I can bring in fresh air as I apply the protective coating. I'm pleased with the space for me to set out my work. She looked up, "Lighting's good."

Gavin brought in a box.

"Help you?"

"Uh huh, trunk's open, car's parked in the close delivery area. All the boxes in the trunk and car come in."

They set the boxes down in the work space assigned to Lori.

"When's the trail for you?"

"JJ said I stay here until you feel secure in what you'll do."

"OK then, set everything out, along with the garden plan from your mom. Thursday and Friday the crew will work on the actual garden off the main trail. By then I should be finished with the wooden signs to go with the little fairies and friends. Last, I'll do the calligraphy for the marker. We'll place that marker at the beginning of the trail."

"I'm removing the carvings from their boxes. Mom, so organized, wrote the carving name outside the box."

Lori held the map as Gavin put down each carving. Each one lay straight and solid.

"How the heck can these stand alone, especially in hard rain, with leaves and twigs from trees near by."

"Bad weather, mom thought about that." He touched a carving, held it up to her. "See, on the back side of each figure she integrated a firm stick so the figure stands up through the rain."

"Ingenious, Gavin, these figures, carved from tough wood."

"Yeah, to last for years, provided they don't get knocked down."

"They're so lovely, all painted. How did she preserve the paint colors?"

"Wood preservative, then special shellac, same substance you'll brush over the fairy garden signs after your finish the calligraphy. Mom created a second set of carvings."

"My gosh," she smiled to Gavin as he set out the last carving. "She worked for years on this project?"

"Yes, years," he paused, an image of his mom appearing in front of him, "she completed the replacement set, painted and all boxed up three days before she got so sick."

She heard his hoarse wavering voice as she went to him. Lori saw a glint of tears forming in his eyes.

"Can I, uh, can I, help, Gavin?"

" A hug, please."

Lori reached up and put her arms around his neck. His arms came around her. They held on to each other.

After a time they let go. He looked into her green eyes.

"Th, thanks for comforting me."

Lori touched his shoulder, smiled to him and returned to the garden map. She set it on the table. With each figure she made certain a sign and the wording for the sign lay next to the figure. Twice more she moved along near the table.

"I'm confident, understand what my writing task is," she whispered to a figure.

Gavin watched her walk from figure to figure.

"Got it, the wording mom wanted?"

She turned to him, nodding, "So much fun, writing, my favorite."

Gavin caught her smile and the glad sparkle in her eyes. She gave him a wave as he walked away.

℀

Lori assembled her writing pens and special ink. She found a stool she could sit down on. She started with Rachel's first carving, touching the beautiful dark-haired fairy. She wore a pink gown and had white wings projecting from her back. She touched the bright smile on the fairy's face. And the fairy had green eyes.

"Wow, kinda like mine," Lori shook her head at the coincidence.

The fairy had her arms open, as if she welcomed a visitor.

An hour and a half later, Lori completed the wording on the fairy's sign. She ran her fingers over the sign, "I'm Flory, a fairy with magical powers. I work for good in affairs of humans."

"Nice."

She propped up the sign and stepped away from the table.

"I can see the writing from a little ways away, writing's the correct size, clear and flowing. I think the cursive, that children will be able to read the writing. Yeah, and the sign itself, it's well proportioned for the size of the carving."

Lori decided when she finished her second sign that she would apply the special shellac to the first sign, to see how it looked.

"Don't want the ink to smear, sure hope it won't," she whispered as she started the second sign.

She gazed at the second figure, a wizard with a tall purple hat and long purple coat. He held a wand. When Lori finished the writing she propped up the sign and stepped back to read it.

"I'm Willem, a wizard who practices magic. I profess to have special powers."

Lori nodded her head, "Yes, I'm satisfied with the writing and a trail walker's ability to read the sign."

After locating the shellac container, she used a small brush to add shellac to the bottom of the sign. She gritted her teeth as perspiration stood out on her forehead. She worked her way up the sign.

"Great, the wording isn't smearing."

Lori stopped and set the sign down. During a break she opened a pop she brough with her lunch.

"Special treat, Lori, today you done good," she smiled to herself, "you deserve this pop."

After drinking it half down, she set the drink aside, a distance from her project.

She completed the other five signs over the next three days. Lori ran her fingers over the signage as she walked from one carving to another.

"I'm Largo, and I assist Flory."

She looked from the sign to the boy fairy. He wore a brown hiking outfit with wings out his back. Largo held onto a tall walking stick.

"Don't know how Rachel captured his expression, but she did," Lori laughed as she touched the wizened face of the grayish-green troll. "Oh what a grump, complete with a frown and turned-down mouth."

She ran her fingers over the writing on the sign, "I'm Gil, a troll, and I protect treasures beneath the ground."

Lori moved on to a darker-skinned girl fairy, dressed in a soft blue gown with golden wings extending from back. She held out her arms, smiling to welcome a visitor. Lori read, "I'm Ara and with my magical powers I too can work for good in human affairs."

She moved to the right and glanced at the boy fairy. He wore a fisherman's gray waders and a soft brown cap over his dark hair. He held a fishing pole in one hand, and he had gray wings on his back. He smiled out to anyone gazing at him.

"I'm Mulray and I use my magical powers to help, that is, when I'm not out fishing."

Lori giggled as she hadn't heard the humor until she read the sign out loud.

"Gotta make sure I mention humor to Gavin. His mom musta been smiling all the time as she created these little carvings."

The gray-colored shriveled old man without a smile, but with a baggy gray long coat, needed a sign. When completed Lori ran her fingers over the calligraphy on this sign.

"I'm Hal, a gnome, a guardian of the interior of the earth."

Thursday morning she began Rachel's wording on the bigger sign she created for the fairy garden entrance. The larger calligraphy took Lori more time. Finishing in the early afternoon, she propped the sign up and stood back.

She read it out loud, "Fairies and their friends welcome you to our imaginary enchanting garden."

Lori shook her head, "Never thought this would turn out so super cool. Wait'll Gavin sees all this."

That afternoon she shellacked the entrance sign three times. And she brushed a final coat of the special shellac on the other seven signs.

℘

Lori gave Gavin a wide smile that Friday morning. The shellac smells tickled their noses. Wide open windows gave the smells a chance to escape. Her excitement grew as he moved from carving to sign. He studied all seven carvings and signs several times. She saw his smile, getting wider and brighter as he touched several signs. Her face heated up as he placed his hand on the table at the end of his visual inspection. Tapping the table twice, he nodded to her.

"Lori, cannot believe how super cool the signage turned out. A gift, you create beautiful, readable calligraphy."

She held her hands against her burning face.

He moved toward her, "May I give you a hug, my thanks?"

"OK."

They hugged and he saw her bright red face as he stepped away.

"Lori, what's th' matter?"

"Don't take compliments."

"Yeah, that really bothers you."

She nodded to him.

He moved away and gazed around at the work bench.

"Mom," he looked up, "think you see us, see Lori working on your project.

Whatcha think? Awesome, right? Wait'll we put the characters in the fairy garden, a special place, dedicated to you."

"Gavin, come look."

She waved him to the fairy garden entrance sign Rachel created.

He traced his finger across the welcome sign calligraphy.

"'Zactly what Mom wanted."

"Gavin, turn the sign over."

He held the wooden sign and gazed at it.

"I see you decided to put the writing bottom right."

Gavin set the sign down and read "Carvings and signs created by Rachel Lundstrum in the 1990's, the fairy garden, her dream."

He stepped back, tears stinging his eyes.

Lori watched him. Hot tears burned her eyes.

"Gavin, had to give credit where credit was due."

"Lori, thank you, so considerate of you to think of mom."

"What now?" she looked into his eyes.

"You decide which character and sign to take up the trail. Hey, they're working on the fairy garden today."

"No, Gavin, you decide which carving. I'm in my trail clothes and have my backpack ready for the rest of my work day."

"Time to pack up the characters and signs for safe keeping. I've designated shelving for the project."

They packed away the trail project within a half hour. Lori left behind several of her special writing pens and ink. JJ mentioned her working on the trail entrance sign during the eighth week. A week earlier the trail workers built the sign for the entrance in the community workshop.

Lori pumped along on her bike, easing toward the trailhead. Gavin arrived before her. They gathered several smaller tools needed for the fairy garden trail. She followed him, just out of his trail dust. Looking around, she remembered her efforts as she helped the crew move forward, creating trail. Lori nodded her head as a feathery gentle warmth surrounded her.

"It's my trail high."

She hiked ahead, closing in on Gavin, "It's the end of Week Five. This where we're supposed to be, with the trail?"

"JJ says we're two days ahead of schedule. But three weeks to go, and rain, I imagine."

"I'm excited to see the fairy garden area."

"What I know, a place off the trail, I think mom would've picked. Anyway she had the location on her map."

"Yay, workers ahead."

Lori's heart pumped pumped against her chest. She jumped up and down, smiling at what she saw. Gavin stood next to her as they watched the workers. JJ whistled to stop work. The crew came and stood around them.

"Guys, Guys," Sophia spoke, "it's gonna be so, well, for the children, come see."

The group walked the curvy path they created that day. It went left and ahead to the right, then curved left again. The path moved left and right until the end. Lori peered up, seeing tall pines and trees bordering, but not overhanging the fairy garden.

"Before we finish the path, I want us to return to the beginning of the garden. I've somethin' I want to show you," Gavin smiled.

They walked behind Gavin. He removed his backpack and took out two bubble-wrapped packages.

"Where's Willem, the Wizard and the second sign located?"

Sophia pulled out her map. She and Sam found the location, the second stop. Gavin followed them with his packages. The group stood close around the three of them as Gavin undid the wrapping. Silence held for several moments.

"Oh, my gosh, a beautiful carving," Raymond whistled.

Gavin took the purple-dressed wizard and placed the thick stick, the back part of the wizard, in the ground. He touched the carving. The wizard stood solid. Then he pushed the thick stick of the sign down into the soil.

A trail worker read, "I'm Willem, a wizard who practices magic. I profess to have special powers."

"Wow, Lori, you did all the calligraphy, on all the signs?"

"Been working on this all week. But I'm glad I am back on the trail."

Clapping surrounded her.

"Lori, you've got a special gift, the writing, beautiful."

Glancing around at the workers she nodded, "Thanks, loved doing this writing."

Gavin pulled the wizard and sign from the ground, rewrapping them for his backpack.

JJ spoke, "On one of our last days of work, we'll set up the carvings and signage, a special time for all of us."

₳

The trail crew created the rest of the second mile of the trail. They planned for three weeks. Stomach flu took one crew member for several days. One Wednesday rain poured for half the day.

The crew met in the community work room that afternoon and the next morning. They completed the signage for the trailhead. Then Lori began her calligraphy. This sign welcomed visitors to the trail, called "Old Rail Trail."

She worked with JJ on the size of the calligraphy for the top part of the sign. After three attempts, and with the guidance of several workers, a decision concluded regarding the size of the writing.

The crew wanted to leave most of the sign empty. A note near the bottom right, "PLEASE LEAVE YOUR BIKES AND DOGS AT HOME; THIS IS A NATURE TRAIL."

Lori spent an entire day completing the writing on the sign. She shellacked this sign four times.

"We're on schedule. On Wednesday Mrs. Langdon will walk the trail with us. She wanted to hike sooner. I told her we were not ready for her. We talk once a week since we began. She's excited, anxious to see our work, supportive of our effort."

He looked around, "Have you all met her?"

JJ saw nods from his crew. And he sensed the anticipation of finishing up. He watched their renewed energy and more smiles this last week.

ℂ

Bree called Lori on Tuesday, the last week of work.

"Miss you, Bree."

"Miss you more, Lori. I lived in calmness with grandmee. Gosh, my parents got commitments. The minister before us began several projects."

"Let me guess, Bree. They ran out of money before the work got completed."

"Lori, you read my mind."

"Yeah, so I can imagine the anger from the congregation, expressed to your parents."

"Uuuggglllyyy."

She heard the harsh tone in Bree's voice.

"Money causes so much heartache, Bree."

"The congregation, sorta like your church members, Lori."

"Whew, oh Bree, your folks, so much on their minds."

"The members, well, the chuch is poor."

"Oh my," Bree heard a sadness in Lori's voice.

"So Mom got a job, works part time in a city office. We need her salary. And it is helpful we speak Spanish. We know church folks and other community members. A few old members speak little English. Dad does short sermons, one in English and another in Spanish."

Bree heard Lori's teary voice, "Girl, concerned, 'cause I didn't hear from you."

"Worked my butt off, in charge of painting both the little church inside and out. Between a good painting crew, all church members, and Dad, we got it done. Now I'm painting my bedroom and another room in the small home we live in. Hey, and it's just a short way from the church."

"So you live where the previous minister and family lived?"

"Uh huh, the home needed cleaning big time, and the painting. In a week and a half school begins."

"Excited, for the change and your new school life?"

"I am, the grinding work hours, done. Homework, a blessing once it starts. My folks express their gratefulness to me often. Uh, they walked into a hot mess. Oh my gosh, I'm whining. The trail."

"Done on Friday. Mrs. Langdon walks the trail with us tomorrow. Completing this project, exciting for me."

Lori explained the work of the last few weeks, the carvings and signs for the fairy garden.

"Oh Bree, extraordinary how I enjoyed the signage calligraphy. And Bree, Gavin, he's special to me. I guess I'm a little gobsmacked. Never had a crush on a guy before. I'm changed, this summer experience, a new way of seeing life for me."

"Enjoy every second of this special time, Lori. He'll be a senior, college plans for him?"

"'Course."

"And you?"

"Looking at what I'm interested in if I decide to go on to school."

"Hey Lori, how you gonna pay for this?"

Lori heard the serious tone of her voice.

"Uh, work my butt off. I saved every penny of my wages for this eight weeks of trail making. Financial aid, yeah, look into that. Crushing debt, I plan on that for years after a degree."

"Girl, go to your counselor as soon as school starts. Georgia's got the HOPE. You might be a candidate for the HOPE. You yanked up your grades as a sophomore. Stay fast to your making top grades your junior and senior years."

"Right, just like we talked."

"But you, Bree, how you gonna pay for school?"

"Uh, never shared. Before grandpa died, he set aside money. He realized my folks could never help, with the kind of missionary work they do. My grandmee, she promised to watch over the finances for me. Job number one now, decide what I want to do with my life. And where I want to go to school."

"Maybe a state school in New Mexico?"

"Uh huh, much cheaper than going out of state. Gotta go, it's so good to hear your positive voice."

"I love you, Bree."

"And I love you, Lori, take care, you all are in my prayers, in my thoughts."

"As you and your family are in mine."

℃ℂ

Gavin came to her as they looked out over the fairy garden. Their trail work almost completed on that last Friday. He touched her shoulder.

"Gavin, makes me cry, so, such a cool place for folks, little children. And you saw Mrs. Langdon, how much she liked the whole area when she joined the crew on Wednesday."

Lori turned her head to him as he looked to her. Gavin saw tears glinting in her dancing green eyes.

"Yeah, I'll come here, talk to mom, her special place, not the cemetery."

An Ony Springs newspaper reporter joined the group later that Friday morning. He shot photos of the trailhead and of workers on the trail. He asked all the journalist questions, the 5W's and the H. As the group approached the fairy garden, the reporter talked to Gavin about his mom's project. And he kept taking photos.

"Hope to give you a front page story, with my editor's OK," the reporter shared with JJ.

"Great PR for our community tourism efforts, appreciate your time and effort."

"Hey, I got it on my calendar to revisit the trail later in the fall. Such a blaze of colors everyone will see among the different trees."

The trail crew shared memories of the trail construction as they came down the trail this last time. Sophia and Lori planned to meet for lunch one day. Lori felt torn between tears and the euphoria of completing this laborious project. She stood, a fixed look around at their creation. She took in the evergreen smells, the new soil beneath her feet. JJ gathered the group. He looked from worker to worker.

"Quite the experience to get to know you and to enjoy outdoor Georgia."

He heard clapping begin as he gazed at his smiling trail workers. He nodded to them after the clapping stopped.

In JJ's choked voice they heard, "There's no doubt in my mind, this is the work I'll continue once I finish my degree. It's instilled such a love of the outdoors in me."

Gavin spoke out, "And I think in all of us, JJ."

Lori watched as the group nodded their heads and murmured their agreement.   The crew hugged each other before they piled the tools they took that day into JJ's trunk.

Gavin whispered in Lori's ear as they hugged, "Thank you for your phone number. I want to get to know you. So good to work with you."

They stood back from each other. Lori smiled into his smoky gray eyes.

She nodded, speaking in her quiet voice, "See you, maybe before school starts?"

3

My dad, Lars, and my mom, Nancy."

"Happy to meet you," Gavin smiled to blonde Lars and dark-haired Nancy, as he shook hands with them.

"When will you be back, Lori?"

They stood together in the Grifson living room.

"A few hours, after we hike the rail trail, we eat at the café on Main."

"Quite an accomplishment for you, Gavin, and for Lori."

Nancy nodded to this tall young man with sandy blonde hair.

"Super hard work, a great eight weeks in the outdoors."

"Mom and Dad, some Sunday afternoon I hope you will hike the trail, see our efforts. You've seen a couple of before-and-after pictures."

"We'll get'er done," Lars smiled to them. "Have fun."

She touched the trailhead sign as they stood in front of it. She passed her fingers over the smooth wood.

"Lots of memories, making this, writing and shellacking."

"Hey, what about the reporter's coverage of the rail trail?"

"Good work, I liked the part of the article about your mom. She made such a contribution to the trail."

"Yeah, accurate detail by the reporter. I got an extra copy of the article. I wrote my grandparents and included the article."

Lori noticed his sad eyes as he stopped talking.

"I haven't communicated much with them since mom's death. They came a short time for the celebration of her life."

He shook his head, "Mom and her folks, not close."

Gavin strode along the trail. He turned his head back toward her.

"I need snapshots of your life, Lori."

"Same for you, I want to know about you."

Lori shared a little of her early days. Meeting Bree changed her life.

"That girl, like an angel, messenger from God. She brought me hope for my future."

Lori paused, not sure what she wanted to say next.

"My appearance, improved, our home, cleaner and picked up, made it look bigger. I take an interest in my classes. I make friends. Sophia and I do spend time together. You and I hike. I continue to be active. A dull slug, yeah, me."

"A dull slug, hey you worked hard at that café," Gavin shook his head. They stopped for a break a quarter of the way up the trail.

Lori confirmed the changes in her life the past year.

"Now you, you've met my family, Christmas Lane, our home."

"My Dad works for Georgia Department of Transportation, a supervisor. Long hours for him as he's in charge of a chunk of north Georgia roads. Mom carried the load with me 'cause we saw dad on weekends and evenings."

"Your mom, Rachel?"

"Paraprofessional in the Ony Springs schools, many jobs for her over the years. What was so great," he paused and smiled to Lori, "she was home when I got home from school. She wanted that life; dad agreed."

"What happened?"

"She got sick, then sicker, 21 days in the hospital. Dad's health insurance helped, but the bills, awful. Then death, he sat down with me. We worked the math. He asked me, ME," Lori watched him point to himself as his forehead wrinkled, "what I would do?"

Gavin saw Lori's wide-eyed look.

"I told him I'm just a kid, but dad, the house, her car, sell 'em."

He stopped talking and took in a deep breath.

"Mom had a tiny life insurance policy and small pension from being a public employee of the state, kinda like dad. So he paid off part of the debt. And he set aside a small amount for me. It might pay for maybe one semester for college."

"Now?"

"In a rental condo, the best dad can do."

He smiled to Lori.

"Debt's gone from the house sale and using savings. Oh, Dad's in a retirement system with the state. That way, when he retires, he'll have a pension coming in."

Lori shook her head, her forehead furrowed, "My folks got nothin' except Social Security."

Gavin scrutinized her, nodding, "Ya know, that means."

"Workin' the rest of their lives."

He nodded. His gray eyes bored into hers.

"Education, Lori, most important for us, for our future. Hey, Bree walked into your life, helping you understand."

"Yeah, the need to study, to learn all I can to carry on. Like your mom, dying, you helping your dad like you have."

They hiked along the rail trail. Lori 's feet lightened as they approached the fairy garden. She started on the path, stopping and kneeling beside each of the seven carvings. Gavin stood at the fairy garden entrance, watching Lori. She moved along, taking in each carving and the wording on the sign beside each one. At the far end he watched her put her arms in the air, and turn around in a circle.

She came back, smiling, "Awesome, all the characters look just as nice now."

"Yeah, and it's been a few days ago. They will hold up well in the wind and weather. Just was talking to mom, how proud I am of her gift of wood carving."

"Gavin, I am happy; I like being here with you."

"I like that you are here with me," he smiled as he turned to her.

Lori tipped her face up to his. She closed her eyes as he caressed her lips. She put her arms around his neck as they kissed again. They stepped back from each other. A sharp jolt hit Lori in her tummy and groin. The ache moved up her body to her face. Her green eyes glittered into his smoky grays.

He caught a breath, "Your eyes, Lori, those pools caught me as I saw you smile on trail that first day of work."

"My attraction to you, that first meeting with Mrs. Langdon at school."

They hiked up, pointing out work they did, together, and with the other group. At the trail end, Log Landing, they stopped. A cool wind swirled around them. They sat, drinking water. Lori shared her special hiking trail mix.

"Uuummm, cereal, nuts, raisins. Yummy mixed together."

Gavin pointed to the semicircle.

"Like the way we stacked the railroad ties, like a half circle?"

"Great, so someone can talk or perform for a hiking group. So lucky that we found those ties thrown off to the side."

"Yeah, so glad thieves in the past ignored them."

"Remember, we found the ties when we cleared the debris."

They moved along at a good speed hiking down the trail.

"I'm drenched," Lori giggled as they stopped at the trailhead.

She wiped down her body with a towel from the backpack.

"I have no idea how we stood the heat, Gavin."

"Got used to it. I didn't think to bring a towel."

He wiped down his face, arms, and legs with his hand.

"Could've lent you my towel."

"Nah, that's OK."

He drove them to the downtown café. They held hands as they walked along. They chose a table so they could sit next to each other, away from the chatter at other tables.

"Practice driving with Nils, he's competent, gives me good tips. My mom will ride with me next. Gavin, I'm so ready to drive."

"Make it to your birthday?" he grinned to her.

She high-fived him, "Yes!"

"I got a job."

"Tell me, Gavin, that's great news," she patted him on the back.

"Yeah, 4-6 Tuesdays-Fridays, longer hours Saturday and Sunday."

"Where?"

"Little hardware store down the street from here. Every penny hasta help."

"Gosh, just see you at lunch?"

"Right."

They held hands as they stood on Lori's front porch. She kissed him on the cheek. He hugged her.

"Thank you, I like spending time with you, fun!" she exclaimed.

She watched his smoky eyes, in that instant become smoldering. He stood back from her, then turned and waved to Lori before he got in his car. She waved back.

As she came into the kitchen, her mom asked, "Fun time, hiking?"

"Mom, what a nice guy, I really like him." Nancy watched her dancing eyes and quick nod. "At 13 he lost his mom. Whew, the medical debt crushed his dad, but they're surviving. Gavin's dad works long hours, so he's on his own."

Nancy moved to Lori and touched her shoulder.

"Gavin's lived a lot of life already, difficult times. Our Lord, He's with Gavin, and with us, always."

&

Lori had purpose as school began in September 2001.

"I want to go on to school. I have a plan," she shared with her folks.

She made an appointment with her school counselor to talk about her plan. And Lori checked the job openings board in the counseling office for possibilities. An elementary school needed after-school help with students. Lori called, desiring a challenge. She interviewed. The school expressed an interest in Lori, with her enthusiasm and wish to help. She got the job. And she started the next Monday after school.

Artwork, snacks, reading to students, playing games, music time, Lori enjoyed every minute of her time at after-school. Fun, she had fun, getting to know a special group of younger students.

$$\mathcal{8}\mathcal{0}$$

"Still need to ride your bike. But before long you will have transportation."

Lars saw the wide grin on his daughter's face.

"Wanta show you the wheels. Should get you through the next two years and beyond."

"I'm so excited." She looked up to her dad, "Can I drive?"

"Yeah, took it for a drive, filled up the tank."

"How's it handle?"

"Fine."

Her dad unlocked the side garage door and turned the light on.

She gazed around, "Oh Dad, what a," she paused, smiling to him, "WOW."

Lori let her fingers glide across the whole side of the sedan. Her nose caught the odor of paint.

"A ton of work?"

"Engine work and I took it in for the repaint. I know good body shop help."

"Dad, the color, silvery gray. It's nice, and I like the two-door."

"And I see your eyes, your question, yes, I plan to work on a fixer-upper for church."

"Thank you, Dad, the car, my future," she went to her dad and they hugged.

"Wanta take it out for a drive?"

"Can we?"

Lori sat tall as she drove.

"I'm confident, with this automatic transmission."

"Good, you started with a stick shift."

She turned to her dad, "This runs so quiet, smooth, not that many miles."

"Belonged to an older lady, who started having accidents, her sight and reaction time. Her kids took the car away. So this sweet set of wheels has had a fender-bender or two. But it's solid now."

"Dad, I gotta pay for gas, insurance, got my job."

"Sweet pea, do the gas, but mom and I will cover insurance. You must save for school. And your high school is aways from your after school job at the elementary school. You gotta hustle to make it."

Lori drove with a 25 mph speed limit the whole way.

"Hard, but I can do this. With a bike, I can make shortcuts."

"You'll figure it out, Lori."

She turned to him and smiled, "A few weeks, yay, my birthday."

"And your license?"

"Right away, hoping Nils can take off and drive me to the DMV."

"No worries, Lori, it will all work out. Very happy that you work at a school. I much prefer that to the café."

℘

9/11/2001

She shivered as she stood with students in the lunchroom. She heard sobbing all around her in the crowd. Her eyes burned from her continual tears. Scenes from the twin towers coming down caused more sobbing. Lori tasted vomit rising in her throat. She swallowed and swallowed. She followed other students out of the building. Schools closed for the rest of that day.

Gavin found her at the bike rack. They hugged and held on. Lori cried,

"God, help us all."

He added, "Never been so sickened or so sad."

As they parted he talked about getting his homework done before work at 4 p.m. Lori's tears began again. She pedaled home at a slow pace.

"No work for me today," she cried aloud.

At home she turned on the t.v., but turned it off just as fast.

"I know what I gotta do."

She wrote a note for her folks and biked to her church. People came and went, stopping by to pray. Lori heard their prayers above a whisper. Her brain circled around the tragedy, not understanding.

"I confess I'm not doing very well, Lord, bless and keep us all."

She whispered that several times. Her head stopped pounding.

"I'm going home."

Lori tossed and turned. She woke at 2 a.m. sobbing. Praying on her knees she blurted out, "God, you are with me, with us all; Lord, I don't comprehend the situation. Please guide us, all of us, through these next days. Me, all of us, must keep love in our hearts, love for God and love for one another."

"I'm sleepwalking, this whole day," she shared with another helper at after- school the next day.

"Yeah, me too, but we have the little children, a comfort for us."

Lori's helpmate nodded to her, "The grief, awful."

Reading time began. Little ones gazed at Lori. Curious George gave children and helpers laughs and a time for feeling safe before the day's end.

&

Gavin sat across from Lori as talk and laughter rang through the lunch room.

He touched the Bible she handed to him.

"Thanks, Lori."

He smiled to her.

"I appreciate you listening to me. You help me talk about God. My folks, never anything like Sunday School, no church service."

"I invite you to church. We go on Sunday. My folks rest that day. Mom works Tuesday-Saturday. Dad fixes a car on

Saturday in the garage.   Both have physical jobs, on their feet. They get exhausted."

Gavin watched her furrowed forehead and heard her serious tone.

"You're concerned about your parents."

"Yeah, I really am."

"I'll think about your invitation. I start work at noon on Sundays."

"Let me know; gotta finish quick, a project to get started in the library."

She saw his wide smile, "Ah, did you?"

"Yeah, to my counselor about the HOPE."

"You'll keep me informed about the scholarship for you?" she questioned as she stood up to leave.

He nodded, gazing into her luminous eyes.

Her mind screamed, "I sure care about you."

As she walked toward the library, she reviewed the discussion with her counselor.   She appreciated the information the counselor shared with her and thank her for the time she spend with Lori. She found the book she needed for her project. Lori sat in the warmth of a peaceful whirling in her mind.

"Apply for the HOPE.   I believe I'll qualify for that scholarship. Better grades, through my whole senior year. The little kids I work with after school; I know what my training and learning need to be."

She exhaled a deep breath and got up to go to class.

ℐℂ

"Lori, I enjoyed my time with you and your family for your birthday."

"I appreciated you coming. It's crazy days. I love driving, leave school, and presto, I'm with children at their school."

"Better than a bike?"

"Yes!" Lori nodded to her.

Today they sat across from each other in the sunny lunchroom. A pizza smell wafted from the serving area.

"Your SAT's, want to share?"

"I tested good, got prepared. Hey, I've worked hard 9-12."

"Where for your nursing?"

"Lori, out-of-state, OK from mom and dad."

"Sssooo lucky, Sophia."

"Wonderful parents."

Lori saw her wide smile. Then she visualized her own folks. They work hard, struggling to make a life for Nils and me.

"So blessed to have my parents," she prayed in silence.

Sophia gazed at Lori, "Your folks are on your mind?"

"They are," she nodded and smiled to Sophia.

℥

That Saturday afternoon Lori held her homework in one hand as she answered the phone. She hurried to her dad in the garage.

"It's George at the café."

Lars wiped his hands on a cloth and rushed in to the phone. Lori's stomach spewed acid as she listened to her dad's responses.

"Mom slipped, a water spill. Headed to the ER. X-rays, of course. You stay. I'll call. Doin' homework?"

"Soon as I'm done with the assignment I'll watch some college football."

She watched as he put his tools away, making the work area neat. She came to him and they hugged.

"God's with us, Lori."

She stood with him at his truck.

"I'm praying, we have medical insurance, right?"

"Yes, the three of us, Nils is on his own. We don't charge him rent here. He pays all his insurance plus helps with groceries."

"When my friend, Gavin, lost his mom, his dad lost most everything."

She watched her dad shake his head, "Medical debt can equal bankruptcy."

"Awful, oh please let mom know she's in my thoughts and prayers."

He patted her on the shoulder.

"'Course I will."

She watched the thin line of his lips.

The phone rang several hours later. Lori rushed to get it.

"Dad, tell me."

"We'll stay with mom. Fix yourself soup and sandwich. We'll go to the cafeteria here. She broke her right leg, the calf, a clean break as she slid into the bottom of a shelf area. She wears a plastic boot, on crutches. Mom got banged up; they'll keep her overnight. She's sore, home sometime tomorrow. Prayers, please go to church, pray for us all. I'm so pleased that you drive now."

"Dad, let mom know."

"Know what?"

"I will work her 7-4 Saturday shift. It's somethin' I can do, to help out at George's.

"Lori, sure about that? And what about your homework?"

"Time management."

"Mom'll be grateful, Lori"

"Family, Dad, oh we are a strong family."

"Yes, we are."

She hung up the phone, walked around the kitchen and sat down at the table. Lori put her head down and thought through this unfortunate accident, what it meant for her family.

"Dad, a terrible burden on him, Mom did well with tips."

She nodded her head, "Whatever I make Saturdays goes to my family. Awful, four other days, no money coming in from her."

Lori stood up and made a strong pot of coffee. She drank a whole cup.

"I'm thinking better, the shock of mom, bad."

She stood tall, all her muscles, well practiced from the summer work. Lori stepped into each room in their Christmas Lane home. She talked out about the tasks to be done.

"Proud of how much better I've helped, more organized. Clothes washing and drying, picking up, vacuuming, sweeping, bathrooms, helping mom with fixing dinners. Those are my tasks. Dad will grocery shop, as always. Leaves, gggrrr, out back, keep them raked up. Number one is studying, getting homework caught up. Mom and dad will agree."

She looked in the clothes hamper in their small laundry room. She estimated two loads and began washing. Lori peeked in on the football game.

"Go Bulldogs," she shouted as the team held the lead.

She ate her yummy tomato soup and and the toasted cheese sandwich. She cooked it in a pan which made the cheese soft. Cleaning two bathrooms came next.

"I want it nice and fresh for mom. I'll keep my messy brother's door closed, so mom doesn't see that."

Lars drank the coffee Lori fixed Sunday morning. He thanked her for the coffee.

"When did you start to drink coffee?"

"After school started, caffeine gives a burst at night for studying.

"Keep you awake?"

"Not at all. Homework starts kinda late."

Lars left, having no idea when Nancy might return home.

℘

Lori looked up to the gray sky, hearing the birds chirping in the trees near the church.

"I'm a little early."

She slowed her pace as she walked to the church entrance.

"Gavin!"

Lori stood in front of him, smiling her wide smile.

"Hello Lori, see," he paused, "I made it."

They walked together up the steps to the church entrance. Lori's eyes swept with tears, her heart swelled, tingled. A grinding ache started in her groin and spread up into her throat. Her cheeks turned bright pink.

"Your folks?"

"Tell you after service. Thanks for coming, Gavin."

He noticed her immediate tears and her bright cheeks.

Lori's prayers held her through the service, prayers for her parents. And she winced several times, her brain aching, at the thought of the financial strain of her mom not working.

Gavin watched her out of the corner of his eye. The service ended. He saw tears welling in her eyes. She took his hand as they left. Lori introduced him to Reverend Candliss.

As they shook hands, the reverend spoke out, "Good to meet you, Gavin. You are always welcome here."

"Thank you sir."

Gavin gazed at this smiling man. He heard the tone of his voice, kind.

She faced him as they stood next to her car.

"Oh Lori, please, I saw your tears at the end."

"Water got spilled on the floor at work, mom slipped, broken leg. Workmen's comp for her, but no work for a time. Crutches, cane, limp, physical therapy."

Lori looked into his sombre gray eyes, "What else," she nodded.

"Your family's finances, oh gosh," he whispered to her.

"7-4 on Saturday, I'll work her shift. It'll all go to family."

She gasped, "That's four days, her not working."

Gavin held her by her shoulders and moved her to him.

The gentle touch of his hug brought a reassurance, his caring.

"Gonna be rough, and holidays coming."

They came out of the hug, "Gosh, hadn't thought of that. Another homemade Christmas, you know," she took in a deep breath, "we've had them before."

Gavin gazed down to her, "I'm so sorry."

She nodded and caught his eyes, "Your prayers, please, need them for me, for my folks. I'll be in charge at home."

They hugged. He kissed her on top of her head.

"Talk at school tomorrow?" he asked, watching her face as she gave him a small smile.

She nodded, "Headed home, the work?"

"Got it."

She watched him as he walked down the street to his car. He turned and waved. She waved back.

"I love you, Gavin," she whispered.

Warmth suffused her body, like a soft blanket wrapping around her. She smiled almost the whole way home.

She heard the phone as she came in her front door.

"Mid-afternoon, Lori. Emergency for the doctor, when that's cleared he'll sign off for mom to come home."

"Done with cooking, just reheat when she gets hungry. Does mom want anything special?"

"Nope, wants us, nearby, in the comfort of her own home."

"Crutches?"

"Hates like heck, how awkward the crutches are. Fast on her feet, that's her, before this."

"Ah," Lori paused, giggling, "knowing mom, she will zoom around soon."

"Not, Lori, she got banged up, one arm and the side of her head."

"Concussion?"

"No, very lucky."

Lori's heart ached and her tummy rumbled as she gazed at her parents.

"I'm so glad you are home."

She hugged her mom.

Nancy stood, using her crutches as she saw her daughter's smile.

"Grateful to be home with you and dad. That hospital, ooowww, just for the sick," Nancy laughed and smiled to Lori.

Lori nodded, "You still got that wonderful sense of humor."

"Uh huh, gotta go on, God's in charge."

"Amen," Lars and Lori spoke out as they assisted Nancy back to their bedroom.

"A shower, my wish on arrival."

"Better, Mom?"

"One thousand percent," Nancy giggled after she joined the family in the kitchen.

"Oh Lori, our coffee so excellent," she spoke out after she downed a half cup.

The meal turned into a quiet celebration. Nils joined them as they prayed for the continual healing of Nancy's leg.

They sat together, enjoying each other's company.

"Toughest for me, home all day, I've not done that since before Lori started Pre-K."

"The guys at the shop said they will give me several recipes for you to try. I'd like that, try different foods for all of us to enjoy."

"Thanks, Lars," Nancy looked from Lori, to Nils, to Lars. "I'll need other entertainments."

"Books from our school library, maybe I can find some for you to read."

"Thanks, Lori, never took the time to read, no hobbies. I work."

Lori noticed her mom's overbright eyes, a little dazed.

"Your pain pill, Mom, time?"

"Right, Lori, I need to lie down. So noisy at night in the hospital, and up early for, like blood work. I'm sore, exhausted."

With Lars and Lori's help Nancy settled on her side of the bed. When the boot came off, Lori placed an ice pack on her mom's leg.

"That will help with my swelling. Thank you both."

"And I'll help you get up and down from the bed, Nancy," Lars smiled to her.

Lori gazed at them as she stopped at their bedroom door.

"There's love here, all around us."

In the kitchen she cleared the table and started washing and rinsing dishes. Lori had a thought that almost took her breath away. She stopped and wiped her hands. She looked up at the sunny sky as she walked around the back yard.

She held her hands over her elbows, "No coat, it's cold."

"This is, my gosh, gonna be harder for mom than I ever expected."

Tears gushed from her eyes at that thought.

"She seems so vulnerable, never seen that side of her. I gotta help, much as I can."

With new resolve she stepped back into the kitchen, drying the dishes and putting them away.

That night after homework Lori wrote a note to Bree to go out the next morning.

> Bree, oh best friend, my mom got hurt at work. It's bad, no work for a long time. Her job is so physical, walking and handling heavy trays of food. I can't wait to see you after Christmas. You MUST come! All A's so far, I can't believe how far I've come, that's YOU helping me!
>
> Gavin, I love him, I love him, my first love. He cares about what goes on with me. HOPE for him, so he'll stay in state. He'll meet awesome girls in college, so I will let him go to the rest of his life. Lucky to know him, thanks to trail work. I gotta write notes to you…expensive to call. And I'm crushed with work at school, don't have time to e-mail you from there.
>
> I'm working Saturdays for mom (7-4 shift). My folks are grateful. Remember how you encouraged me…still got the little ones for after-school camp weekdays. Counting the days until we see each other!
>
> Love, Lori

Gavin joined her for church three times. That Sunday he took her hand as they walked from church.

"Lori, I see the strain, in your eyes. I sense you are tired."

She turned and nodded to him, "Gag," she paused, "exhausted, slept in until 7 this morning. Crazy at work, we serve breakfast on Saturday until noon. We got the brunch eaters, big time."

"Thanksgiving next week, better for you?"

"Yes, school for two days, Wednesday – Friday I can relax. Mom's starting to help, does a lot of the evening meals. I don't get home from after-school until 5:45."

She took his hand and held it in hers. They gazed into each other's eyes as they stood at her car.

He shook his head, "So sorry I'll be gone."

"Being with your dad, and then seeing your grandparents, maybe a reconciliation? It's gotta be tough, being estranged from folks you love."

"Hey, you shared about your grandparents, Lori. Complicated, our families sure are."

She nodded to him, "For certain, are you driving?"

"Yes."

They reached out to each other, hugging a long time.

"Whew, so glad to be on break, happy time for me."

"Another hug, please, come here, bright eyes."

They stayed in the hug.

&

"Homework accomplished, and it's just Tuesday evening. Nice job, Lori."

She patted herself on the back.

"No more homework for almost a week, yay!"

She slept in until 7:30 the next morning, "Wonderful" she shouted as she got out of bed. Her dad promised to start the coffee. That way Lori and her mom could have coffee together.

They sat at the table, sipping their brew.

"So awesome, I slept in. How're you sleeping?"

"Still can't get comfortable at night. To the docs at 10:30. I do have a secret."

Lori scooted closer to her mom.

"Tell me," she whispered.

Nancy spoke in a quiet voice, "Starting to put a little weight on my gimpy leg. I work on that during the day."

"And the feeling?"

"Not much pain, but stiff."

She patted her mom on the back, "That's great, Mom."

Lori turned to her mom as she drove them to the clinic for the checkup. She watched her mom smile.

"X-ray, I expect that, see how I'm healing."

"I'm confident; everything's going OK. You are strong, Mom, all your years on your feet, lifting trays of food."

"Uh, say something?"

"About putting weight on that leg?

"Uh huh."

"Yeah, I'll hear what he has to say."

≠

Later that afternoon Nancy took the turkey breast from the freezer. Lori stood across from her, pouring the pumpkin pie mix into the pie crust.

"Ready for the oven," Lori spoke out.

She smelled the pie, the cinnamon and nutmeg spices tickling her nose.

"In you go," she noted the time when the heat needed to be turned down and how long the pie needed to bake.

"It'll be our simple meal, Lori, the breast, potatoes, salad, rolls and pie. Dad's doin' the best he can with food budgeting. I'm so glad he's always been the shopper."

Lori stepped to her mom and gave her a hug, "Me too, Mom."

"You'll hear from Gavin?"

"Yeah, he'll call me sometime Thanksgiving Day, a long drive home."

"I'm happy you'll hear from him. Oh, and thank you for the ride today to the doc. I appreciate all that you have done to help me heal."

Lori touched her mom's hand, "Happy to see the X-ray, and hear the report on your recovery."

Nancy eyed her daughter, "A little sad, long time 'til the first of February, when he says I can return to work at the café."

"Mom, the doc wants to make sure you're really healed, doing your exercises, and handling the increased walking he's asked you to do."

ℳ

"Happy Thanksgiving, Lori."

"And Happy Thanksgiving to you. Thanks for your call. Uh, how's the visit?"

"Dad's holding his tongue; we're leaving tomorrow. Think dad and granddad acted glad to each other at first. They just don't get along."

"Guess you know how blessed and lucky you are, you know, the pleasant relationship you have with your dad."

"I am blessed, like you say. Crazy busy, it'll be that way at the hardware store. I'll be working long hours over the next days." He paused, "Oh Lori I am thinkin' of you."

"And I think of you, lunch on Monday?"

"Yes, I like being with you, even for just a few minutes."

"Same, safe travels, take care, Gavin."

ℳ

"Mom, dad's workin' in the garage for a little while. I want to hike the rail trail by myself. OK if I go for a few hours? Chores finished. I'll start the pizza 30 minutes before we eat."

"Uh huh, go, have fun, Sophia coming?"

"No, other plans, I'm happy to do the trail by myself, wonderful memories of last summer."

She let her mind drift as she drove to the trail head. "Making money and learning and using my body, a great time working."

Hiking Sunday afternoon helped Lori review the past few days, the crazy day yesterday at the café, and the pleasant church service that morning. Her thoughts circled to Thanksgiving Day. She kept her strong stride up the trail. She gazed all around her at the welcoming setting, some trees with orange and red-tinged leaves still hanging on.

"Thank you Lord, for our thanksgiving yesterday, and for every day. I'm pleased 'cause mom continues with her recovery. Dad, his auto shop gave him a raise. Pretty sure his boss doesn't want to lose his most valuable mechanic. My steady big brother, Nils, hey, he's getting more responsibility at his station. Maybe there'll be more pay for him. His boss lets him handle quick fix stuff."

"And me," she whispered, "I keep asking You to guide me." She nodded, "It's working now. School, good, the little kids in after-school care, fun, and Saturdays, oh George, he asked me if I wanted work fulll-time this summer. I know You'll help me decide what to do."

She stopped, held onto a tree near the trail and bowed her head.

"Dear Lord, Thank you for my life, for my family, and oh, for my friends."

4

Lori walked toward him as he sat in the noisy lunchroom, two Mondays after Thanksgiving. Her head buzzed like a working chainsaw as she watched his wide smile.

"Yup, I know," she spoke out before she got to the table.

She plunked down hard as she sat across from him. He took her hand.

"Georgia Tech."

They squeezed hands and held on.

"Your dream school, Gavin, the HOPE?"

She watched his eyes cloud for a moment, then clear, "Gotta see my grades coming up, but it looks promising for the HOPE."

"Almost all straight A's, that oughta do it, right?"

He nodded to her, "Gonna be engineering, not sure which major, but Tech's got so many programs."

"Your job, stay for the summer?"

"No, going full time all summer. I've learned a ton of practical stuff working at the hardware store. But I'll be looking for engineering internships summers after this."

"That'll help you decide on what you'll wanta do with your degree."

He nodded and smiled to her.

"I'm happy for you, Gavin."

"Thanks, Lori, I know you want the brightest future for me, like the future I want you to have."

She squeezed his hand, "So many students you'll meet, so many experiences you'll have, it'll be great!"

He watched her eyes dance as he heard her excited voice.

ⅎ

Please, Lori, can you come to my home this afternoon. It's important that I talk with you."

"Two p.m. work for you, Betty?"

"Perfect, see you then."

Lori checked with her mom. The call came in after they arrived home from church.

"Good that you didn't ask why she wanted to meet with you. She wants privacy, and you will give her that. I'll keep Bree and her family in my prayers."

"Me too, Mom."

Lori and Betty hugged after they greeted at Betty's front door.

"Smells, wow, uuummm!" Lori exclaimed.

"It's called wassail, an English drink. I fix several batches every holiday season. Bree and her folks love the stuff."

"Here, let's sit at the kitchen table. There's always activity in the backyard, I see squirrels, birds, an occasional hawk zooming through."

Betty poured hot wassail for Lori and herself.

"Oh Betty, the brew tastes as good as it smells, cinnamon, and several kinds of juices.

"I've written out the recipe for you. It's super healthy for us."

"Oh, thanks for this recipe, I gotta make it for my folks."

"Do that, you'll be surprised!"

"Oh gosh, when'll Bree and family be here?"

Betty indicated the dates, which Lori repeated.

"I can't wait."

Lori clapped her hands and gave Betty a wide smile.

"Your folks, your mom?"

"Mom improves every day, no job work until February. It's killing family finances, just dad's salary. I work at George's Saturdays, gotta help out."

"That's right, I had lunch with friends, saw you there on a Saturday. It looked like a crazy day for you."

"It was," she smiled to Betty, "I wrote Bree. I haven't heard back." She shook her head, "I'm so worried. And I see by your sad eyes, oh, somethin' going on."

Lori couldn't help it. She started to cry.

"You are a very observant young lady."

"Please tell me."

Lori touched Betty's arm, "Share?"

"Bree dust-mopped the church floor and sanctuary. Her mom found her unconscious at a side aisle. The mop lay on the floor. Bree regained consciousness in the ER. The hit she received caused a concussion, a terrible headache."

"Good, oh my gosh, she, attacked?"

"Yes, hit on head from back, she did not see her assailant. That's what she told the police when they interviewed her, several hours after she regained consciousness."

Lori watched tears form in Betty's eyes and dribble down her cheeks. She stood and moved around to Betty's chair. Lori sat down next to her. They hugged. Betty cried and cried.

The sick pain in her stomach ached, like when Lori heard Trey's screams on the rail trail last summer.

"Want to talk about it?"

"Awful, Lori, awful."

Lori waited for her to begin.

"The concussion, not the only damage to Bree's body. She was raped, vaginal area torn, blood; she's a virgin."

Lori paused and spoke out, "She didn't see the attacker, oh dear God, Betty, I'm so sorry."

She tasted vomit in her throat. Lori succeeded in choking it down. She continued to touch Betty's arm.

"Pray, I'll pray for Bree, her family and you, each day as many times as I can."

Silence held between them for a little while.

Lori looked Betty in the eye, "OK, I got it, I understand why I haven't heard from her."

"They're still coming."

Lori clapped her hands, "Hurray, wonderful, I'm so looking forward to seeing my own angel, the messenger who helped me bring positive changes to my life."

"There's more, but first I want to have a snack, and more wassail. How much longer can you stay?"

"At least half an hour, then home to help with dinner and finish my homework."

"School, for you, Lori?"

"Doing so good; gonna try for the HOPE."

Lori watched Betty's smile, her dimples showing, "That's wonderful."

Betty poured more hot wassail for them and set out the oatmeal raisin cookies.

"It was Bree's first intercourse, and, oh Lori, she's pregnant."

Betty's tears came again, igniting her tired and irritated eyes as Lori watched her.

"Bree's a super strong person. How's she getting along?"

"Remarkable, moving on with her life."

"She gonna stay in New Mexico and have the baby there?"

"No."

"Abortion?"

"No, Lori, I'm helping her."

"Oh my gosh, how?"

"She'll come after Christmas with her folks, but she'll stay here in Georgia. She won't return to New Mexico."

Lori shot a puzzled look to Betty.

"Found an accredited boarding school for unwed mothers, where Bree can finish her junior year. I'm paying for her tuition, room and board."

Lori questioned, her eyebrows raised.

"Yes, the school has a religious affiliation. They work with an adoption service. Bree wants the baby to be adopted by a couple desiring a child, a mixed-race child."

Lori thought it, then spoke it, "But, but she doesn't know, you know, the race of the baby's father."

"Correct, right now, well, we're black, so at least knows half of the child's origin."

Betty went on to share the name of the school and the community in Georgia where Bree would live until the baby came.

"After that, what about her senior year?"

"She wants to return to her parents and help out in the New Mexico community where they have another year's commitment to their church."

Lori's head swirled with questions…Bree, her commitment to her family, and what about the crime?

"Who knows about what happened to Bree?"

"The medical staff, the hospital she stayed one night, their family doctor, police, and a minister, a family friend. She's a protected minor."

Lori nodded to Betty, "Sure as heck hope she's protected, the whole privacy thing."

"Bree and my son and daughter-in-law still struggle with what's happened. They remain very vigilant."

"Their church locked up except for services?"

"It's been since the attack."

"Help?"

Betty nodded to Lori, "Another minister in their town counsels them. Bree and her folks, well, their anger and sadness are easing. Remember Lori, my son, he's done counseling with this very situation. He never thought it could happen to his own flesh and blood."

They sat together, saying the Lord's Prayer and holding hands.

"More prayers, Betty, I'll continue to pray for Bree and her family. I just have such admiration for Bree. She's so strong; she'll make the changes she needs to make."

Lori found her coat and the card she wanted to give Betty.

"Thanks for sharing; I wanted you to have this card I made myself. It's a bit of artwork I love doing along with the calligraphy."

Betty tore open the envelope and put her hand on the outside of the card. She traced around the gold-colored outline of an angel. Betty opened the card. She whispered Lori's calligraphy and then spoke out, "There are angels among us and you are one of them."

At the bottom of the card she saw, "Love, Lori."

"Oh Lori, stunning."

She smiled into Lori's green eyes, "You have a God-given gift."

They hugged.

"Bree knows I'm talking to you about what's happened to her. She would never give you that kind of news when she arrives."

Betty handed a card to Lori, "The recipe for the wassail."

"Can't wait to see my special friend, my best Christmas present, for sure."

Betty nodded to Lori at the front door, "Mine, too, darlin'."

℘

Lori shoved the pizza into the oven. She turned to get the salad makings from the frig. Her tears came and a gut-wrenching pain kicked her stomach. Lori got to her bedroom and closed the door. She envisioned Bree, standing with her big smile and her shining dark eyes, and everything Bree helped her with in this small bedroom of Lori's.

She lay down on her bed, "God, someone I love carries so much pain, what, God, what," she paused as she cried into her pillow, "what now for Bree?"

Nancy moved down the hall at her slow pace, using her crutches, but putting a tiny bit of weight on her leg with the boot. She heard crying. She knocked on Lori's door. She got no answer. Then she heard crying increase. Nancy opened the door and walked to Lori as she lay on her bed.

"Lori, oh honey, what can I do to help you. You're crying so hard."

Lori sat up and hugged her mom after Nancy eased down on the bed.

"Mom, can't talk about it, no, it's not about me. Somethin's happened; I'm just so upset. Really, I will be OK, time," she stopped and took a deep breath as she got a grip on her emotions, "God's in charge, his plan."

"That's right, Lori."

"Gotta take the pizza out in a few minutes. I'll start the salad."

"I'll help you," they hugged again, "and Lori, let me know when you're sad, at least I can hug you, now I know you're troubled by stuff."

        ⌓

"Let's meet at church, the Sunday before Christmas, OK?"

Gavin watched her approach his car after he arrived in the parking lot. As he got out, she gave him her wide smile.

"Oh dear one, you have the shine back in your eyes. Whatever bothered you, it seems better."

"So happy you're here, Gavin, I'm more myself, upbeat, positive."

They hugged and held hands as they took steps into the small church. Lori noted the donated red poinsettias from church members, sitting on the floor in front of the altar. The congregation seemed small that morning. Lori wondered, hoping that a crowd might appear for Christmas Eve.

Reverend's sermon, short and to the point about finding the joy and peace of Christ's birth, helped her keep up the calm she prayed for since she learned about Bree from Betty.

"I liked what reverend had to say, Lori. I'm glad I came and met you here."

They walked to Lori's car.

"No homework, so great," Gavin breathed out.

"Yeah, a whole week with just work and relaxation. Business at your store, it'll slow down?"

"That's right. Dad and I have a invitation from friends to have Christmas dinner with them. I'm gonna hike the rail trail a couple of times during the week, when I'm not at the store. Bree will keep you busy?"

"Fur sure, so excited to see her. I will try to bring her to the store so you can meet her."

"Great, I want to meet this girl who's helped you change your whole world."

Gavin watched as she shook her head and now tears glistened in her eyes.

"I, I, my folks, hurtin' so bad."

The two of them moved and leaned against her car. He put his arm around her shoulder.

"I bought a tiny tree, got an extra big tip from a family Saturday morning. So I bought the tree, decorated it."

She stopped talking and they hugged. Lori's tears flowed down her face.

"You OK?"

Lori shook her head.

"Will be. Oh, mom, she's been doing too much. She's now taking our advice, spending more time in her bedroom reading. I've picked up cooking all the meals again. But it's OK, no school and no after-school job. Each family member is buying food as part of Christmas dinner to share. Nils bought the ham and is baking that. I made a black forest cake. Mom and dad will fill in other stuff."

"Duh, what's black forest cake?"

He watched her wide smile and a spark in her green eyes.

"She's better," Gavin decided.

"So my version is a chocolate layer cake with cherry pie filling between the layers, then dark chocolate frosting. Oh, I add almond flavoring, half a teaspoon full, to the cherries, makes them taste awesomely delicious. We fur sure gobble down that cake."

"Yummy," his eyes bored into hers. "So I know your money deal." He nodded to her, "Learn all you can. Good grades will help you with scholarships."

"Thanks Gavin. Pray for me, best present you can give me. "Hey", she looked up into his eyes, "I care for you, so much."

He held her eyes, "I love you, Lori; God bless and keep your family as your mom's leg continues to heal."

Gavin closed his arms around her. He kissed her on top of her head.

She stepped away from him and smiled, "Merry Christmas, Gavin."

"And Happy New Year to you."

She moved to the back of her car to observe him walking to his car. He turned back before he got in. She gave him her signature side-to-side wave. He nodded back to her. She stood, frozen in place.

"Yes, I did hear him, he, he told me he loved me. And, oh gosh, I didn't say anything back to him. I love you, Gavin."

She unfroze and unlocked her car.

"How long have I cared for you, Gavin?"

The idea raced around in her brain all the Christmas holiday.

"And he told me he loved me, loved me."

"I find that incredible, hard to believe," she whispered as she stood in her kitchen, gazing out the window at her back yard. She followed a squirrel jumping from the ground up onto a low tree branch.

She heard the phone. After the call she walked back and forth in her living room.

"Bree, I'm disappointed that I won't be able to see you 'til you get back. I know grandmee wants to show you and your folks your school. It's gotta be the best situation for you."

Lori plunked down in front of the small Christmas tree after that.

"Even you, little guy, have that evergreen smell, like being out in the forest."

A sad tingly upset raced around in her tummy.

"OK, tree, I'm speaking to you. I had so many plans for Bree and me. Now just one trail hike, want her to meet Gavin. She needs to see my mom."

She took in a deep breath and exhaled it.

"Grow up, Lori, I will face many disappointments in my future. Courage, Bree's got huge courage, marching forward through some tough stuff."

Lori took the mail from their mail box the day she would see Bree. She looked at the return address on the letter she got from her high school.

"Aha, grades," she shouted out.

"Oh Lori, wow, congratulations!" her mom exclaimed after Lori showed her the grades.

"Will be able to apply for the HOPE, Mom."

Nancy hugged her daughter.

"College, possible now with financial aid, sure, we coulda' never dreamed you'd be able to go on to school."

Lori picked up the call.

"We're back, Lori. Need a half hour to settle in."

Lori left early. She drove to Bree's grandmee. After she parked her car away from the Newland home she walked several blocks for a few minutes.

"Can't believe how nervous I feel," Lori breathed out as she shook out her hands before ringing the doorbell.

Bree opened the front door to greet Lori.

"Bree, finally to see you."

They hugged and jumped up and down, their special way of greeting each other.

"My folks, Lori, Rob and Marie Newland."

Lori shook hands with these folks who stood in the background as Lori and Bree greeted each other.

"Hi Rob and Marie, heard so much about you, like I know who you are already," Lori smiled to them.

Bree's folks laughed with Lori.

"Uh huh, just like we know who you are. You are about the only thing Bree's talked about for weeks."

"We're goin' for a walk; be back in an hour or so. Lori and I, we got a lot."

Bree paused.

"Go you two," Betty spoke out as she waved to Lori.

"Such a special area, the stately homes, and gosh, holiday decorations everywhere."

"That's why we're out here, Lori."

"Talk, I got nuthin', great grades, trying for the HOPE next fall."

Bree nodded to her. They stopped and gave each other a hug, then walked along, linking arms.

"Grandmee, found this, just," she paused, "appropriate school. It's accredited in Georgia. My grades for this upcoming semester will count toward college. The school showed us their wait list for families who want to adopt. Amazing the number who'll take a mixed-race child. More want boys than girls."

She shook her head and turned to look into Lori's eyes, "Do not want to know the gender."

"Bree, we think alike, who's gonna pay for medical care before baby comes?"

"Grandmee and my folks take care of that, there's insurance."

"Hospital, for you and baby?"

"Adopting family, baby goes immediately to them. It's part of this adoption contract."

"Bree, tough question, see the baby after birth?"

Lori heard a soft cry from Bree.

"Nothing, just ask for a picture to keep, right after clean up."

"What about any communication?"

Bree turned to Lori as they stepped off the sidewalk for a moment to cross the street.

She touched her shoulder, "The adopting parents have the right to explain the situation to the child. At 18 he or she is free to contact me through the adoption service, but not until then. Lori, an abortion, I thought about. Hate, it was hate, what happened."

Bree burst into tears. They walked a little. Lori turned to Bree and hugged her. Bree grabbed onto her friend and they hugged until Lori thought she could let her friend stand alone.

"God, oh God, He doesn't want me to destroy this life inside me. Just such terrible circumstances of conception."

They stood, looking into each others eyes.

"Dear God, Bree, this child in you deserves to love and be loved, His wish for all of us."

After they nodded to each other and hugged again, they walked along. They stopped in front of a home decorated with all white lights inside and out. Even the white wreath hanging on the front door expressed holiday cheer with its bright red bow.

"I'll do a special look at the adoptive parents. My wish, the baby goes to a college-educated couple. They might not be able to have children. What would be ideal is a couple who're willing to take a chance on the unknown part of the baby's genetics."

They returned to walking, admiring more homes with their outside decorations.

"You ever seen these streets at night during the Christmas season, Lori?"

"Uuummm maybe once or twice, with mom and dad when I was younger. Exhaustion for them after their work, they go to bed early. And they start work early."

"Want you to come to dinner with my grandmee and my parents. Then mom and dad hafta get back to New Mexico."

"How are you feeling?"

"Honest?"

Bree looked at Lori.

"Yeah, of course."

"'Cept for no periods and expanding boobs, I'd never know I was pregnant, no morning sickness. I have a flat tummy. Fall semester I had difficult classes with homework, lots of it. Still had the home chores, like when I lived with grandmee."

"Ship shape, as always, right?"

"Absolutely."

"There's a best part, wanta hear?"

"Yes," Lori held Bree by her shoulder as they walked along.

"More people join our church, since dad took over. Dad's a nice man, a friendly guy, and he reaches out, to people in town, and to other ministers. He organized an ecumenical effort the night after 9/11. Our church overflowed with folks from all over our town, from different churches. Dad gave an encouraging talk, folks caring for folks, moving forward, forgiving, not hating."

"And since then?"

"Oh Lori, we're REALLY known, a friendly little church that reaches out to folks. We gave holiday food baskets to five church families, folks really hurting."

"Yeah, our church does that every holiday time."

"Your dad, a car this year?"

"He did. The need came in very late, for the holidays. But my wonderful dad pulled two all-nighters. Nils helped, but dad sent him to bed. He starts work at 6 a.m."

"The family?"

"Single mom, three kids, unbelievable what happens in some families."

Lori nodded to Bree, "The woman's got a job, so with the car to drive to work, well, I believe they'll make it."

At the Newland home Lori stopped Bree before she walked in.

"I pray for you, Bree."

"Zactly what I need."

They looked into each other's eyes.

"I'm strong, and I'll face what God sends me. I will go to college, that much I know."

Lori put her arms around Bree.

"Thinkin' of you; you're never alone, Bree, remember that."

The next day Bree met Gavin at the hardware store. Bree visited at the Grifson's and saw Nancy. She demonstrated her walking abilities and praised Lori for stepping up to help the entire family through her healing time at home.

Betty invited Lori for dinner before her son and daughter-in-law left for New Mexico. She saw the same caring and concern for folks in what Bree's parents shared with the family and her that evening.

Lori hugged both of Bree's parents and Betty as she got ready to leave.

"God bless and keep you folks as you return to New Mexico. I appreciate Bree so much. She continues to make my life better, through all the examples she's given me. And you know that I love her."

Bree's mom struggled with tears at Lori's words.

"You take care, Lori. God continues to bless you," Bree's dad spoke out as he smiled to her.

As she drove down several streets in the Newland neighborhood she again enjoyed the different lights on the homes, some with white lights and other with colored lights.

"So special, everything's stunning here."

She drove into her own neighborhood with its tiny homes, a few with front porch lights on and almost none with holiday lights.

"There's love here," she whispered as she walked up to her front porch. The front porch light shone into her eyes. She patted her front door before she put her key in the lock.

"Oh mom and dad, I thank you for the porch light greeting for my home."

℘

"License, got it quick?"

Lori turned back to Bree, "The day after my birthday."

They clapped and Bree let out a cheer, "Go Lori!"

Bree watched Lori hike ahead of her on the Rail Trail. She gazed around at the evergreens and the leafless trees. The smell of decaying leaves tickled her nose.

"Uh, I don't have mine. Couldn't face a process like that. I had to heal from the assault, maybe next summer."

"When for the baby?"

"End of May, I think. School year mostly done. Grandmee will come and I'll stay in Ony Springs until the doc tells me I'm OK for New Mexico."

Lori stopped and turned around, "What'cha think?"

Bree nodded, "The trail, nice, looks like it'll hold up good. It's just what I think. I'm no trail expert."

"Hey, ahead, want to show you."

"Here's the backstory for my folks back in New Mexico. I'm in Georgia to help out grandmee, who's part time this semester, medical stuff. I'm doing school this semester in Georgia, correct?"

"Right, helping out with grandmee."

They strode along.

"Oh, Lori, the bright afternoon sunshine, the glistening pines with their green boughs, what a feast for my eyes."

"We're almost there."

Looking ahead, Lori viewed the fairy garden off to the left.

"Take your time, I'll do housekeeping, pull twigs and stuff from the fairy path."

Bree bent down to read the fairy garden sign. She turned and smiled to Lori, "Oh," and then she paused, "oh, my."

Lori watched her walk from the fairy to the wizard and then to all the other carvings. Bree read the signage as she went along. Lori stayed out of her way. She walked a circle around the outside of the fairy garden and picked up twigs the wind might scatter over the garden.

"Well planned," Lori spoke out as she gazed up to the open sky.

Not a single tree blocked her upward view. She watched the pine trees standing guard, back aways from the garden.

"A delight," Bree smiled as she walked back to the start of the fairy garden.

"My feeling exactly, this whole fairy garden, and, oh, the trail goes another mile."

"Lori, I'm doin' good. It's cool and refreshing. Hey, I just got so much admiration for the work you all did on this trail, amazing," she nodded her head to Lori.

"A huge amount of work, the trail, we didn't expect that, I mean the work load. Those who stayed on, talk about getting in shape, really incredible."

"What about heat, humidity?"

"Everybody lost at least five pounds, got stabilized, learned how much water to drink during the day."

"Superb, the calligraphy on the signs, very readable, even for grade schoolers. How did you work out the writing on the signs?"

"Uh, 'bout half way into our trail work, our boss, JJ, asked me to complete my writing at the community work room, four busy days for me. The group worked on the entrance sign and I did the calligraphy on it. I shellacked all the signs, trying to preserve the wood and the writing."

Bree looked at Lori, "Girl, you have a talent, that calligraphy work. You had jobs from the terrific ability?"

Lori nodded, "Several commissions, so fun, but next year, no way. My school load, way intense, so much to learn, and makin' grades."

They hiked to Log Landing.

"Yeah, this is the end of trail for now."

Bree gazed all around and saw the railroad ties.

"I like what you did with the ties, hikers sitting around in this big semicircle listening to a speaker, or to, oh gosh Lori, a guitar, or a Native American flute."

"Only can imagine the possibilities, Bree."

Lori and Bree exchanged bags, trail mix and dried apricots. They ate and drank their water.   They listened to the wind singing through the empty tree branches way back from where they sat. Silence held between them as they descended the trail.

"This whole time with you, Lori, perfect."

They hugged. Lori took them back to grandmee's.

"I'll walk you up. You got precious little time with your mom and dad before they leave. And when, your school, Bree?"

"Tomorrow morning, soon as my folks leave."

"I'll miss you."

"I'll miss you, too. Write, OK?"

Bree stood at the front door, trying to smile. Lori saw tears.

They hugged. The lump in Lori's throat kept enlarging. It ached like a furious kick. She stepped away from Bree and turned, hurrying down the front porch steps. Lori moved three steps down the path to the sidewalk, then stopped and turned around. Bree smiled through her tears, blew her a kiss, and waved. Lori blew Bree a kiss, waved back and watched her go into grandmee's. Tears flooded her face.

She got back in her car and put her forehead on the steering wheel. The ache in her throat started to go away as her crying lessened. Lori picked her head up.

"I'm gonna do this same thing when Gavin goes away to Georgia Tech. Get used to it Lori, your little world's gonna spin out. You're going into a college world, somewhere."

She started her car and turned to see Betty's lighted garland twining the front porch railing. She waved to the home. The goodness of the warm and wonderful family inside seeped into her body.

Lori took in the quiet of her own home after she let herself in.

"Mom's resting," she whispered.

She sat down in front of the twinkling multi-colored lights on the little tree.

A peace wrapped around her, holding her. The calm held all through her Saturday at the café. She walked out of work that day, ready for her next semester, anxious to get started.

"And I'm missing the little children I watch over," Lori whispered.

❧

A cool and cloudy afternoon in January awaited Lori as she met Sophia for a run at an Ony Springs park.

They hugged and did their stretches.

"I ran cross country, don't know if you've ever thought about running. Lori, you're certainly built like I am, tall, lean. Uh, I bet you're fast. You ever run before?"

Lori laughed as they finished their stretching out.

"Like I ran around in the café, done a ton of miles in that place. The trail, we hiked and worked our tails off, creating the trail last summer."

Lori loped along behind Sophia after they started their running. She sped up, passing Sophia. They repeated the running loop. Lori did not feel her feet touching the ground. She sped up some more, moving far ahead of Sophia. She ran the loop again, the cool breeze ruffling her pony tail and soothing the skin on her legs. Then she heard it.

She slowed down and concentrated on the sound. Sophia shouted to her, to stop running. Lori lessened her pace and finally came to a top. She breathed deep and leaned over, putting her hands on her hips.

Sophia caught up with her, touching her shoulder.

"Lori, oh my gosh, have you any idea how fast you ran?"

She shook her head, "Nope, never ran like that before. It's so good to stretch my muscles, musta had a kinda running high, 'cause for sure, most of the time, I didn't even feel my feet touching the ground."

"You're kidding."

Lori watched Sophia's eyes widen in disbelief.

"No, that, pure fun."

"I'm telling our cross country coach about you. I'm the fastest girl runner on the team. You smoked me like crazy."

"Really?"

Sophia nodded, "Uh huh, you oughta be runnin' with my bro, Charlie. He's super fast, on the cross country team."

"I did not connect you with him. He's so easy on the eyes; girls're over the moon for him."

"Uh huh, but he's lookin' for a special girl. I told him he'd meet that kind of person in college, somebody smart as heck, driven like him."

She looked at Lori, "You've never met him?"

"No."

"Gotta fix that, you two would be good together."

5

"Hey, Sis, can I sit down with you guys?"

"Sure."

He sat opposite Lori and held out his hand.

"I'm Sophia's little brother, Charlie, nice to meet you, Lori. She's been tellin' met about you, newly discovered super runner."

"Hi Charlie."

His strong handshake tingled clear up her arm. She turned her head to Sophia as they sat in the noisy lunchroom.

"You told him?"

"Oh yes, I shared with him about runnin' with you."

"For reals, you didn't know how fast you ran?"

"Nope, it's like I'm carried along on a breeze just above the ground."

On Sunday afternoons Lori and Charlie now met at a cross country route the high school team used. On the third day Sunday they ran Lori slowed down. Charlie stopped them half way through this run.

"You're slower, you OK?"

"Work Saturdays at George's café; crazy day, busy, ran my legs off. Let's sit down, please."

She turned to him as they sat.

"Mom broke her leg at work. Healing, rehab, she's a long-time waitress at George's. I take her Saturday shift. It's killin' our family, her not working. The Saturday pay and tips I make, helps our family."

"I didn't realize. Don't know much about you, 'cept for the running and you being Sophia's friend. After our run, could I meet you at the little café on Main?"

He watched her wide smile and shining green eyes.

"I'd like that, only an hour 'cause I got homework. I didn't get it finished after work last night."

Lori perked up after their talk. Charlie slowed down and let Lori pass him.

"See ya," she waved as she flew by him.

As they approached the parking lot, Charlie ran alongside her.

"For sure, you gotta run cross country with us in the fall. I'm playin' soccer for the high school right now."

Lori patted her face and neck, wiping away the sweat before she headed into the café. Charlie got there first. He sat at a booth waiting for her. She sat down across from him. She blew strands of hair from her forehead, hair loosened from her ponytail while they ran together. He noticed her pink cheeks and Bulldog sweatshirt. Her eyes held him.

"You've got extraordinary eyes, pools right into your soul, Lori."

She gazed at him as they exchanged a bit of their family histories.

"Sophia's decided on her school."

"Oh yay," Lori gave him a bright smile, "Where?"

"U. of Iowa, nursing program, it's what she hopes for."

"Any reason for that location?"

"Yeah, my grandparents, Dad's side, live in Iowa City. So there's family close. It'll be good for me, hoping for Notre Dame, in South Bend, Indiana. So Sophia and me, we'd be sorta close to each other."

"All I remember is she mentioned she could go to school anywhere she wanted."

"Correct, our folks, they made sure we're covered for university expenses."

"Oh Charlie, that's," she paused, "outstanding."

She smiled, nodding to him.

"So, what's in your future?"

"Sophomore year I met a girl new to our school, Bree. She helped me so much, an honest to goodness angel."

She smiled.

"Your eyes, Lori, bright with hope."

She nodded, "I'm making grades, want the HOPE scholarship, maybe UGA. Hey, I never dreamed of I'd be saying those words."

They gave each other eye contact, "Sounds like Bree, a messenger from God?"

"That's right, that's what angels are."

Silence held between them as they drank their coffee. Lori heard the sounds of folks talking around them.

"Hope we can run together again, Lori."

"Me too," she nodded, "Sunday afternoons're only time. We got church in the morning. On weekdays I work after school at the elementary school, after-school base camp."

"Do you like it?"

"Love little kids, never been around them, never babysat."

"Me, always on an athletic field, or runnin' somewhere. I'll walk you to your car."

They each paid for their coffee.

At her car Charlie smiled to her.

"It's good to talk to you. I'm so used to getting hit on by every hottie girl around. Crud, it's a curse to have a good face. I keep my hair cut short, military look. Hey, you sure know how to work." He nodded to her, "I see that work ethic, in your running. Thanks for taking the time for a pleasant conversation."

"Runnin', awesome," she nodded to him.

80

In March Nancy Grifson got approval to return to the café.

"Stay in bed a bit in the morning," Nancy nodded to Lori as she helped her with the salad that Friday night.

"I'll try, but Saturday's I'm used to being at the café at 7."

"Special treat, Lori, you helped me, helped our family, by working that day. It's time for you to unwind a little. You still have your after-school kids. Ah, and you'll have more time to study, make those grades, learn all you can."

Gavin called Saturday morning and asked if he could see Lori.

"I'll have coffee ready, come by. I know you gotta be at work by noon."

When Gavin arrived he said hi to Lars in the garage. Then he and Lori sat at the kitchen table. He looked around the clean neat kitchen and drank some coffee.

"It wasn't always this way, right Lori?"

She nodded, "Bree, she helped me so much."

"How's she?"

"Busy, school, projects, you know, junior year."

Lori swallowed hard. She thought of Bree, soon to have a baby and studying in all her classes.

His eyes met hers.

"Lori, will you come to prom with me?"

The shock of the request left her speechless.

Moments later she remembered her manners.

"Yes," he saw her wide smile.

"Prom, oh how wonderful. I've never been to one, only dreamed about the dancing, for many years."

"Uh, I've never been either. I'm not much of a dancer."

"Fun, it'll be fun."

She watched him, a hint of a smile forming on his lips.

"Thanks for accepting. I know you see another guy."

"He's just a running buddy. I want to try out for cross country, the school team next fall."

"Work?"

"Not sure, in the fall I gotta make super grades."

She looked into his eyes, "And you, the pressure'll always be on at Tech to keep the HOPE up, every semester, you gotta make grades."

"I know I can do it," he nodded to her.

They held hands as she walked him to his car. He caressed her lips with his.

She stepped back from him.

"I ache."

"And I ache for you."

They nodded to each other, eyes connecting. Lori returned to her porch and went in without looking back. Before she closed the door she heard him drive away.

⇣

Lori wrote Bree a note, knowing that Bree kept busy with school and her advancing pregnancy.

"I shouldn't say anything about prom," Lori thought, "'cept Bree wants to share in my joy. And I want to share in her life."

She decided to write Bree about Garin asking her to prom. She needed Bree's advice, about a dress. She had zero money for a dress. Her mom just got back to work. Lori looked at the Thrift Shop. She saw one possibility.

Lori put the note in the mail.

"So selfish, Lori, you are so selfish, look at the tough time Bree will encounter, and it came about prom time."

Lori cried in bed, several nights in a row over that.

Betty Newland called her about a week later.

"Find some time; we're going shopping."

They agreed upon a store, and date and time.

Betty hugged Lori as they met outside the store.

"Bree and I chatted, Lori."

"What's up?"

"I will help you find a dress for prom; Bree insists. She can't be here," Betty smiled to Lori, "except in spirit."

Immediate tears came to Lori and the lump in her throat started to gag her. Betty took her hand and squeezed it.

"Let's go in, see what we find."

Lori tried on several dresses, and tears came to her eyes again.

Her thoughts whirled, "Prom, never should have mentioned it to Bree."

"Betty, do you think Bree would approve?"

Lori stood at the full length mirror and twirled around in the pale blue dress.

"Perfect."

As they walked from the shop Betty spoke up, "Let's go have coffee at the little café nearby. We'll catch up about Bree."

They sat across from each other at a booth away from hearing the front chatter.

"Thank you, Betty. Your kindness in helping me, so wonderful."

Lori patted the dress box next to her and gave Betty a wide smile.

Betty asked if Lori had heard from her granddaughter.

"No, I sent one note."

"And you, Lori, how are you?"

"Making grades, so school's going well and mom's working again Tuesday through Saturday. I don't work her Saturday shift anymore. George wants me full time this coming summer. And Gavin, Betty," she paused an gulped, "he's a boy I like a lot. Prom, a dream I could not imagine I'd ever be a part of."

"I'm so excited for you. Please, if you could take a picture to show me after?"

"Of course, we have a little camera. I'll capture a shot."

Betty smiled, "Bree, doing well, gained just 16 pounds. Her doctor's pleased with her weight. She's finishing a rigorous semester at her school."

She touched Lori's shoulder, "Just like your tough semester, my dear."

"Most of all, Bree's staying positive. Just a matter of time and she'll be here with me. Then she'll return to New Mexico, for her senior year."

Lori looked Betty in the eye and nodded, "I pray for Bree, all the time."

"Thank you, so do I."

&

"You are my beauty, Lori."

She looked into Gavin's eyes as they slow danced to the DJ's choice of songs.

"Handsome, Gavin, you in your tuxedo. It's magic, to be here with you, a dream of mine, accomplished."

A blue light moved in a circle around the hotel ballroom as he escorted her to their table.

"That light casts a spell around this grand room."

"Around you, Lori."

She watched his eyes brighten.

He nodded and smiled, "I'll start at Tech the week after I graduate. No wages, decent ones, around here. Summer school tuition is cheaper than regular school year."

His eyes widened, "I'll prove to myself I can handle the grades to keep the HOPE."

"No work at the store, a relaxing summer?"

He shook his head, "I'm anxious, am moving on with my life. Do you know how special you are to me?"

"Yes, oh Gavin, you have so many new people to meet, experiences to have. And right in the middle of Atlanta, a lot going on. I'm super excited for you."

Lori smiled to him, "Let's dance, in celebration."

They finished their sugar cookies and punch. And the rest of the evening they danced, every dance, fast and slow. He held her close as they stood at her front porch.

"Precious one, I got jangling hormones, confession time."

"Me too," she turned her head into his shoulder.

"We have so much in front of us."

"I love you, Gavin, you're in my thoughts and prayers."

"I love you, Lori."

They kissed long and slow, tongues touching, minds whirling with coming changes.

&

Gavin and Sophia graduated. Lori enjoyed the ceremony, mindful of next year for her.

"I'm a little scared, for what comes after that."

Both Gavin and Sophia requested she attend their graduation parties. She stopped by Gavin's first.

He hugged her, "Glad you came and please introduce yourself to my grandparents. I'm helping Aunty with cake cutting."

She exchanged pleasantries with both sets of grandparents. Genetics sure did not lie. Gavin looked like a much younger version of Rachel's dad.

Lori said so, "Sure can tell you are Gavin's grandpap, the loving term Gavin uses as his name for you, sir."

"Yes, Lori, when we're all together, it's always a point of discussion. Don't know if you've seen a picture of Gavin's mom, but she's a beautiful lady version of my wife and my combined genes."

"I have not; I'll check with Gavin about that."

Lori ate the delicious chocolate cake with whipped almond-tasting icing. She left her card at the entrance table, along with other cards. She found Gavin, hugged him, and added her congratulations.

"Going to Sophia's next."

He nodded and smiled to her. She thanked Gavin's dad and let herself out.

Sophia's family lived on the outskirts of Ony Springs.

"Goodness," Lori breathed out as she saw the mass of cars parked along both sides of the roadway.

She parked a block away, grabbed her clutch with her card and took long strides to the home.

"Never been in this neighborhood," she whispered.

A tall and very pretty woman shook her hand as Lori walked in.

"I'm Lori Grifson."

"And I'm Clare Garrault."

Lori shared about the rail trail she and Sophia helped build.

Clare smiled, "And Charlie, he tells me you are quite a speedy person."

Lori giggled, then nodded, "I guess I am."

"Welcome, please go in and enjoy yourself, you'll find the kids mingling."

She found her way to the table with cards and added hers. She turned and watched Sophia approach her.

They hugged and Sophia stepped away from her.

"You look wonderful, Lori, your hair's so lovely curled on the ends. Somehow it helps emphasize your eyes."

Lori blushed a sunburned red.

"Congratulations, Sophia."

"So excited, headed on a graduation trip with my grandparents. They asked where I wanted to go. Remember last summer and trail building?"

Lori nodded.

"We're part of a volunteer trail crew, building a brand new trail in the Grand Tetons."

"Oh wow, Sophia, that's spectacular, soon?"

"Next week, be gone most of June. August there'll be school."

Lori shook her head, "You won't be here much."

"We'll get together, when I'm here. Lori, we gotta keep runnin'."

"I'll do cross country, if they want me."

Sophia touched her shoulder and smiled, "Oh my gosh, they'll want you; you'll help them win meets, definitely."

Lori mingled with students from several of her AP classes. She watched as Charlie excused himself from three girls vying for his attention. He walked over to her.

"Punch, snacks, cake?"

"'Course; how're you today?"

"I just escaped; would rather be with you. What they want is to have me on their arm, for show."

"Are you just a little bit stuck up?"

Lori glared at him and wrinkled her forehead.

"Yeah, I am," he nodded, unsmiling. "Thanks for your honesty. Refreshing to be with you, my runnin' buddy."

They found the lone table outside in a corner of the back yard. They sat across from each other, putting their food down.

Lori gazed around the beautiful area, lush with trees, pink flowering bushes, and manicured grass.

"What a magnificent place," Lori nodded to Charlie.

"Never seen your hair like this, gosh, you're," he smiled to her, "beautiful."

"Different from the old pony tail with hair hanging out."

"Oh yeah."

"Next year, it's us, graduating."

"Uh, a big party like this next year for you?"

He shook his head, "Last elaborate party, Mom."

"Talk to me."

"I'll do soft talk. Dad's overseas, business trip. It's deliberate, Mom doing this while he's gone."

Charlie watched Lori's questioning eyes as she shook her head.

"It's over, for my parents. They hung together for as long as they could. But, it's finished."

"None of my business, but?"

"You need to know. Dad's moving into a condo he used to rent out. It's three bedrooms, two baths. This place, it's gotta be sold. Mom will stay here until I graduate. Don't know about her, after the house sells."

"One day at a time."

"Yeah, Lori, God's in charge."

"I'll pray for you and your family. I'm blessed to have my loving and caring family, a lot of love in our humble abode," she nodded to him.

"So lucky, Lori, a ton of money between my folks, with their great jobs, but money can't buy love." He paused, his forehead furrowing, "It's pretty much what tore the family apart."

"So sorry, Charlie, you're covered for college?"

"Sophia and I, all set, my folks made sure of that."

"That's great!"

"We're Catholic, our priest will help out, you know, with counseling. It's a tough situation, in every way."'

"Oh gosh Charlie, you said your mom would sell the home after you graduate. Is she staying in town?"

He shook his head, "Don't know, don't think she knows. A new job somewhere else, she's gotta look at her age situation. I know dad'll stay in town."

"Your dad?"

"I'll see him every other weekend, unless he's out of town."

"Hey, you can always talk to me, like we're doing now. God's listening to us."

"I know He is, thank you Lori, to me you're starting to play the angel role that you say Bree played with you."

They put their empty drink glasses and plates on the tray on the patio.

"Hey, beautiful boy," two girls sauntered toward Charlie and Lori.

The teens smiled to them. Charlie got carried off, one girl taking his right arm and the other taking his left. She stepped away from them. He turned his face back toward Lori and shook his head. She noticed no smile. Lori found Sophia for their hugs and goodbyes. They promised each other a run after her trip. Clare and Lori hugged.

"A lovely party for Sophia, thank you," Lori exclaimed as she smiled and waved goodbye.

"So happy to be going home, to my happy home," she spoke out as she walked away.

She made coffee and set her books around her on the floor of her bedroom. Her plan, studying for finals began. The studying continued day and night, until the next Thursday. She finished her exams and went to her little children. She promised herself to get to the running area as soon as she could. On Saturday afternoon she found the time.

"I gotta run," she spoke out as she parked her car in the area where the cross country team ran in the fall.

Lori ran and ran, losing count of the number of times she ran the long loop.

"I'll be ready in the fall. I must run as often as I can."

℘

"6 a.m. until after lunch crowd, Wednesday through Sunday. Can you handle it?"

Lori swallowed hard and bit her tongue for a moment.

"I gotta have this job," she told herself.

She nodded her head to George, "Of course."

Walking from the café to her car she whispered, "Afternoons and evenings free, until bedtime. That's good for me."

Betty called a week after Lori's school year ended.

"Bree's baby belongs to the adopting couple. She's so relieved. And God, she feels, is assuring her the child is in good hands."

"Whew, Bree can go on with the rest of her life. I've been concerned about her but that's all I could do," she paused, "pray."

"You're a senior now?"

"So happy, Betty."

"Picking Bree up tomorrow, she's feeling good, physically and emotionally, wow," Lori heard Betty blow out a deep breath and her voice cracked, "been through, so much. She'll stay with me five days. I'll drive us to New Mexico. I'll stay there as long as I need to. I want to see her settled in her home, and starting to readjust."

"Her grades?"

"Great, now about you, Lori?"

"A's, my GPA is inching up to where it needs to be. I enjoy school, my classes and my teachers. I learn all I can. It's so fun; Bree helped me change my attitude."

"Yes, my dear, attitude is everything."

"I'm off Monday and Tuesday. I work early shift, home about 3:30. Please let Bree know, so we can have time together."

℘

"Keep the Bible?"

"'Course, Gavin, may it give you comfort…for the tough spots in your future."

"I'll miss you," Gavin held her close as they stood on Lori's front porch.

"And I'll miss you. I'm glad we saw the movie together, seems to make our leaving each other easier."

"Hey, we'll be together during the holidays next Christmas. I will finish fall semester before I come home."

Lori looked up into his gray eyes. He held her gaze, then caressing her lips with his own. They kissed. Lori ached, like an explosion, in her heart and in her groin.

"Let him go, let him go," her minds screamed.

"Good luck and God bless, Gavin," she whispered to him.

"To you also, carry me on, along with my love and my prayers," he kissed her on top of her head, "for you."

She heard the choking in his voice. They hugged and she let herself in with a key. She turned and smiled up to him. Tears studded their eyes as they nodded to each other.

Once inside her throat engorged as tears continued to stream down her cheeks. That night she cried, and prayed for Gavin, that school would go good for him. At 2 a.m. she surrendered to sleep. At 5 she woke and began work at 6 a.m. At 2 p.m. she dragged.

"You OK?" her mom whispered to her.

They placed their orders with the cook.

She shook her head to her mom, "Nope, no sleep until 2."

"Gavin?"

"Mom, my first love, ooohhh, it hurts."

She watched her mom smile and nod an understanding.

"Time," her mom added.

℃

Bree arrived in Ony Springs with grandmee. Lori saw her next evening after her return. They sat near each other at the kitchen table, having lemonade and oatmeal raisin cookies.

"You look just the same as last Christmas, Bree," Lori smiled to her.

"Back to my old weight; my breasts're slowly returning to normal. I exercised like crazy as soon as I could after the birth. I tried jogging, like it, gives me kinda a high, moving along with the breeze against my face. I want a flat tummy. Can you help me with sit-ups?"

"Of course, whenever you can start."

Bree took out a picture, "Knew you'd ask."

Lori touched the picture, "Lots of dark hair, gosh, tiny."

"Putting away the pic now Lori, in my safe place. You're the only person to see it, except grandmee."

Lori patted Bree's shoulder and nodded, "Keep it in your safe place."

"My school year at the adoption location, I did real good." Bree eyed Lori, "And you?"

"I, well, I'm pretty sure the HOPE will be mine."

"I plan to apply to both New Mexico and New Mexico State."

"That's good, cheaper to start in state and then a possible transfer. Any idea what you want to do?"

She shook her head, "Not sure, you know how grateful I am for grandmee. She's stepped up big time for me. I've asked her if she's got enough, you know, savings, to still help me with college. She's assured me she's doing OK."

"Grandmee planning to teach a few more years?"

"Yeah."

"Bree, I've thought so much about you and what happened. Counseling about the attack?"

"Uh huh, a minister back in New Mexico helped me through the initial sadness and anger. Then later, here at the school in Georgia, there was another girl, she got attacked, like me."

"Both of you got counseling?"

"We did, and we helped each other. Anger, hate, it grabbed us hard, for the attacker. It got better. Evil, it's present in our world, manifesting itself in many ways. We loved the babies we gave to their adoptive parents. We hope the parents will cherish their babies. From the destructiveness of evil, love comes."

Lori leaned over and gave Bree a hug. Tears studded Lori's eyes.

"I, I," Lori broke down and let out a small cry, "I been praying for baby, for you. And I'll keep praying, as baby grows up. I'm so close to you Bree, dear God, I feel like this kid is my own."

Bree gazed into Lori's teary eyes with tears in her own.

"We both, we gotta let go."

"Boy or girl?"

"I did not ask; everyone there in the birthing area kept their mouths shut. I did not see the baby after its birth. I learned everything was normal."

"Yeah, whatever that means," Lori spoke in an exaggerated tone.

They both laughed.

"Hard to explain the depths of my feelings, around this whole birth situation."

Lori added, "Yeah, I'll share, I got way down in the dumps about Gavin leaving. He's my first love, away at school, but still in my heart as he will always be. Mom said just one word to me, 'time.'"

Bree nodded and smiled to Lori.

ಬ

Late the afternoon before Bree left for New Mexico with grandmee she and Lori met at Lori's running park. Bree jogged along at a slow pace. Her stitches still tingled from the birthing. Her breasts bounced heavy as she jogged. It took Lori five seconds to blast ahead of Bree.

"Unbelievable," Bree breathed out as she moved along, "Lori, fast, must be a natural."

She heard breathing and steps behind her. As the boy started to pass her, he spoke out.

"You gotta be Bree. Lori told me you'd be coming with her. I'm Charlie. Lori and I run together."

"Hi Charlie, uh huh, she told me your're fast. See you at the end."

"Uh huh, see ya."

She watched him zoom ahead. Bree figured he'd catch and surpass Lori somewhere ahead. Lori warned her about the humid heat. She stopped and sat in the grass away from the running path. She gulped down the water she carried. This time she walked at a slow pace to the starting point.

"Gotta work to get back in shape. So great to be outside with nature, sunshine, and the trees," she whispered.

Within 20 minutes Lori and Charlie met her at the starting place. Bree found out Charlie's older sister, Sophia, and Lori worked on the rail trail and became friends.

Charlie told them goodbye and sprinted to his car.

"Whew, Lori," her eyes widened and she smiled to her, "mighty fine looking dude."

Lori turned to her and nodded, "The girls, extremely attracted to him."

"But, he really likes you, Lori."

"Uh huh, we run together, and we talk. He's got huge struggles to overcome his senior year. I'm a friend to him, like you are a friend to me. He's just himself when he's around me. Super pressured by his folks, to make grades. His folks count on him to go to Notre Dame."

"A divorce for his folks?"

"Yeah, can't say nuthin', but it happens sometimes when the kids go away to school."

They walked to Lori's car. She looked across to Bree, "I, uh, I can't figure, oh, you got a sense of what's goin' on with people."

"Remember, I, my folks, too, we work with distressed folks of all ages, all the time, kinda like a special sense of knowing when folks need help"

ℰℐ

The high school cross country coach ate lunch at George's in August. Lori waited on him.

"Lori, I would like you to try out for cross country. I hear you run fast."

She smiled, wanting to jump up and down and shout, but she contained herself.

"I'd like that very much, Coach."

She did try out, made the team, their top female runner. The joy of running, that stayed with her as she worked her last shift, the Sunday before school started.

"What'll I do with all my time, not workin' every second?" she thought. "Ooohhh, yeah, I got school, homework and practice for cross country."

She took orders, brought out food, remembering her folks. She realized how understanding her folks were. They wanted her to have the cross country experience. Her folks did not know what a capable runner she was. Lori shocked herself in being able to run fast. A hard truth caught her up.

6

"I'm behind, I mean, I didn't really study or learn a lot until my sophomore year."

Her counselor offered suggestions. Nights in August and September Lori studied the ACT and SAT prep books, in addition to homework. She needed to be ready for exams in October.

"I have my application completed and mailed to UGA, and to be safe, to Georgia State University,"

Her mom hugged her and her dad patted her on the back when she shared that information with them. They shook their heads and smiled to her, "Well done!"

⳧

Lars watched his daughter run at a Saturday meet. He took the time off from working on a car in his garage. Excitement and smiles came from other parents he saw standing at the finish line. He caught that contagious spirit around him. This meet had teams from five different schools. He watched as eight boys crossed the finish line.

Then he saw Lori. She ran neck and neck with a girl from another school.

Parents and runners who completed the run hollered and clapped as they all saw Lori approaching. The other girl ran across the finish line one step ahead of Lori. They flew by and began to decrease their pace, ever so slow. Soon they stopped. Lori leaned over to catch her breath and put her hands on her hips for balance. She raised her head. Team member patted her back.

103

"Congratulations, Lori," they shouted.

Lars came to her. His eyes teared as he looked down at his red-faced sweating daughter.

"Wow Lori, you ran so well, I had no idea!"

They hugged.

"Dad, oh dad, I'm so glad you got to see me. Maybe some day, mom can see me run."

He held Lori's hand as they walked back to the crowd cheering the team members coming in to the finish line. Ony Springs placed third at the meet. Lori represented the school as the next-to-the-top girl runner of the meet.

Coach looked left and right at his team, "You gave your all, thank you. It's what I expect every time we run."

The team cheered, whistling loud after coach spoke. Lori and her dad headed for their car. Lori watched Charlie approach them. They hugged as they told each other, "Great job."

"Charlie, this is my dad, Lars Grifson."

Charlie grinned wide as he shook hands with Lars.

"Mr. Grifson, I get a sweet charge out of runnin' with your daughter. She's fast and doesn't get tired."

"Good to meet you, Charlie. Yeah, we had not idea about Lori's speed. Hey, I saw it for myself today."

He smiled as he turned and looked down to his daughter.

"She's a speedball."

"Yes sir, she is."

Charlie said his goodbyes and ran on to be with two girls who waited for him.

"Looks like he's got lots of admirers."

"Uh huh, he sure does. Superior looks, that's what interests them."

"Your don't see his looks, I mean you know what's inside him, what goes on in his mind?"

"Right, Dad. He's got tough stuff ahead of him, besides going away to school."

"You'll help him, like you got help from Bree?"

She watched him look at her with wide eyes questioning her.

"I will, Dad."

∾

Charlie planned to visit Notre Dame with his mom in October. At the last minute his mom got assigned a project that would not allow her to go along. His grandparents would pick them up at the airport where the shuttle plane came in.

Lori got a call from Sophia.

"Mom can't come with Charlie; he's a little embarrassed to ask, so I will, 'cause I'd like to come over from school and see you. Would you fly in with Charlie to visit Notre Dame, be with his grandparents and me?"

"I, I could check with my folks. I know we don't have a cross country meet this weekend. It would be a shame to not use the plane ticket."

∾

She and Charlie took Friday off from school and flew to an airport not far from South Bend. His grandparents and Sophia picked them up. They took a tour of the campus by car.

"We're both Notre Dame alums," Vickie Garrault spoke up as they wheeled around.

"Tomorrow we'll walk the campus early, 'cause we know Charlie's never been here. Lori, we took Sophia on a tour of the University of Iowa during her senior year. For now we need to meet alum friends at the hotel where we're all staying."

Sophia and Lori had a room together. She shared about life at Iowa, the hard classes and fun activities of college. The next morning Lori saw the beautiful campus and heard the stories Charlie's grandparents shared of their time at Notre Dame. They found a church with a 4 p.m. Saturday service. Lori attended mass, first first experience in a Catholic church. After early breakfast the next morning the grandparents and Sophia took Charlie and Lori to the airport for the flight back to Atlanta. Charlie's dad drove them from the airport to Ony Springs.

Memories of the weekend flooded Lori's mind, only the second time she traveled on a plane. She listened to Charlie and his dad.

"Dad, gotta let you know, I'm scared out of my mind about going on to school, the university experience. Maybe I need to sit out a year and work. I appreciated that I got to see the campus and spend time with Gramps and Gran. They shared a couple of experiences from their time at Notre Dame. Thank you for me being able to see the school."

"You are welcome, important that you had that experience."

"I'm working hard, planning on being admitted."

He reached across and patted his dad's shoulder. He saw his dad's smiling profile.

Lori kept quiet until Charlie's dad drove down Christmas Lane.

"I'm grateful for this opportunity to see Notre Dame with you, Charlie. And Mr. Garrault, thank you for bringing me home."

Charlie carried her bag to the Grifson front porch. They hugged and stepped away from each other..

"I can help you prepare for Georgia, give you a feel for what we'll encounter, the learning we'll accomplish. I'm so happy you came. You are a friend."

She watched him smile to her as she gave him a thumb up.

"It'll be a great practice, before the meet next weekend."

"Absolutely," he nodded to her.

He got back in the car.

His dad spoke up, "You surprise me, Charlie, she's a special friend to you."

"Yes she is, Dad."

"Not what I expected, son."

"Yeah."

Charlie smiled to his dad as their eyes connected.

℘

"We're gonna be late for the bus, come on, Jesse."

"Yeah, yeah, I hear you in the back seat, Carlo, I'm steppen' on it."

Charlie's body slammed against the left side of the back seat at the acceleration.

"Hey, Jesse, uh, not too fast," Angie spoke up in a warning voice.

Charlie watched as Jesse moved to the left lane to pass the big rig.

"We must leave, I'm sorry, but the four missing teammates won't make this meet," Coach shook his head to his cross country team.

During that meet in a neighboring school district Lori wondered about Charlie, about the missing teammates.

She asked herself over and over, "What happened; this scares me. Goosebumps cover my arms and legs."

"The course, awesome, whatcha think?" she asked several of her teammates as they waited for the rest of their squad to finish up.

"Great course."

Lori saw their smiles. She took first place for women with her time. Their school finished second place overall. And they missed four teammates.

Adrenaline kicked in for Lori, and stayed with her and the jubilant team on the way home. The running high she carried on a run stayed with her as she got off the bus. The noisy team gathered around their coach, smiles and claps going all around. Their high school principal and a school counselor approached the group.

"Congratulations," Mr. Nunroe shouted out. "I hear you did super today. Thank you for your efforts."

The team cheered, some jumped up and down, and smiles came on their faces.

He waited for the group to calm down.

"I have other news. Let's all go over and sit down in the grass. I want to talk to your for a moment before I let you go."

Lori looked around after she sat down. A chill surrounded her as she watched team parents make their way to the team.

She saw her mom who still had her shift at George's. Lori winced as a sick cramp hit her gut.

"Stuff, not as it should be," she shook her head as she whispered.

Nancy Grifson sat down in the grass near Lori. She wore her waitress uniform. Nancy held her daughter's hand. Mr. Nunroe called for quiet.

"Four teammates did not get on the bus for the meet. You all know that. What you don't know is what happened to them. I've been to the hospital with our sheriff and the state patrol. Jesse drove, Angie in the front seat, Charlie in the left back seat, and Carlo in the right back seat. Yes, an accident," he paused as Lori heard his voice start to break. "Charlie broke his right arm. Carlo is in intensive care. Jesse escaped with a slight concussion, giving few details. Angie died on impact."

The group erupted. Lori heard shouts and screams. Her eyes burned as tears slid down her cheeks.

"Dear Lord, protect us; we are in Your hands," Lori kept saying as Nancy hugged her, rocking her back and forth. After a time the group quieted as the principal explained the accident.

"Jesse drove fast, trying to get to the bus in time to leave for the meet. He started to pass a big rig. Then he saw the car heading toward them. He moved the car to the right to avoid a head on. His car's whole right side slammed against the rig. The rig tried to get over on the very narrow right shoulder. The vehicle heading toward their car reduced speed and moved to the left shoulder, avoiding a head-on impact. The driver of the rig escaped unharmed. The three people in the car with the almost head-on got shaken up, but no injuries, emotional trauma for all."

"Angie, Carlo and Charlie, their Catholic church has a gathering tonight at 7 p.m. The Presbyterian minister will be there, Jesse's minister. We'll let you know about Angie's arrangements as we learn them."

Someone asked about charges being filed against Jesse. It wasn't clear to Mr. Nunroe what would happen. Then the group dispersed.

In her mind she saw Charlie from a distance. His face looked devoid of emotion. He shook his head, and Lori shook her head back to him. She looked again; Charlie disappeared. She continued to cry, an achy pain seizing her body. The pain whirled all around inside her. She pictured her teammates, losing a life and the trama of injury. Charlie reappeared, battered and broken.

"Gotta let this go," she whispered.

Nancy held Lori's shoulder on the way to her car.

She continued to tremble.

"Will you be OK getting home, Lori?"

Lori saw her mom's face, her lips thin, and her forehead wrinkled. Nancy still cried from the news.

"I will be, Mom. Thank you for coming. I know you gotta get back to your shift. Will he keep you late?"

"Yeah, probably," her mom nodded. "You fix dinner for you guys. I'll eat at work."

Lori and her mom hugged at Lori's car. She waited a few minutes, for cars, including her mom's leaving the area. She took deep breaths as she decided how to handle the rest of that afternoon.

"Lord, help Charlie, hope it's a simple break, help the families of the other three students. I didn't know Angie, except from cross country. Whew, she ran like a wild breeze."

She stood in the kitchen, chopping lettuce and cucumbers for a salad. She smelled the pork chops bubbling in the oven.

"It's ready," she called to her dad and brother.

They asked about the accident. Lori explained the little she knew.

"We're a smaller team." She gave her dad and brother eye contact. She smiled, "We'll be OK."

"Glad to hear that," Nils spoke up.

"How'd it go with the car you'll fix up this year."

She watched her dad nod his head, "Nils wanted to drive the fixer-upper from the next town over, back to our garage. So I drove my pickup."

A look of concern crept into Nils' eyes. Lori saw his frown and wrinkled forehead.

"Dunno, think this may the most rehab dad'll have to do on a car."

"Got a family picked out?"

"Yes, the car'll need to be ready just after Thanksgiving. The dad works a distance from town. They need two cars, to get kids to school and the wife to work."

Lori looked from her dad to her brother.

"You two, angels, helping folks."

They smiled to Lori.

"Charlie, what'll happen; he can't stay on your team, can he?"

"Right, Nils, he'll need rehab for his arm. He wants to play soccer in the spring. There's baggage he's gotta deal with now, besides the trauma from the accident."

They watched her shake her head, her eyes downcast.

"Be his friend, like you been since you two started running together?"

"Yes, Dad, I will continue to be his friend. I'm hoping he'll get back into a school routine. He's walkin' in my shoes, just took his College Boards. We must make superb grades these next two semesters, spring and next fall."

"That's to qualify for admission?"

"Exactly," she nodded to her brother.

ℛ

Lori watched the girls standing around Charlie at lunch that Monday.

"Yup, vying for his attention," she nodded her head as she listened to the students, quieter than usual.

The pall of sadness, like a dense fog, wrapped around the halls of the high school. Lori heard no boisterous clammering from students as they changed classes. The principal shared the accident at the start of first period. He let the students know that they could seek counseling at school and from several people brought in from the community to help students with their grief.

Coach met with the cross country team. He explained the meet coming up Saturday. He gathered them in prayer for their teammates. Jesse faced charges, no specifics. Carlo went by Flight For Life to a trauma center in Atlanta.

Charlie broke two bones in his right arm. His choices for surgery included shoring up his arm with rod implants, or no surgery. The arm would heal up. He chose no surgery. That came with the warning about being careful about falling. Charlie did everything right handed. The bummer, written school work would be taxing. A memorial service for Angie would be late Saturday afternoon at her church.

Everyone looked at coach.

"Yeah, the meet will get over so you can head back for her service, if you wish to attend. Oh, her folks will bury her ashes in a family plot in upstate New York. That's where Angie's family's from. That will happen at a later time."

"Coach Grant, uh, do you think Carlo's gonna make it?"

Coach stood silent as he gazed from one set of eyes to the next. They saw his tears.

"Can't answer that, Ben. Talking to his parents by phone from the hospital, his brain trauma, very serious." Coach paused, "That is, if he survives."

"Thank you, Coach, for your words."

"Team," Ben spoke out, "We got runnin' to do, for four students who're in our hearts and minds."

Ben moved his arm to the left and his other arm to the right.

His voice trembled and cracked, "They're runnin' right beside us today, and every day the rest of our cross country season."

Tears splashed down on Lori's cheeks as she kept up her fast pace out on the track.

"Don't know how we're gonna do this, for the meet. We just gotta run, for them," she spoke out.

ℒ

I'm not sleeping, Lori."

"Yeah, the trauma, the repetition of the accident, it's always in your head, right?"

"Exactly, over and over, all night long."

Lori stood near Charlie at the start of the cross country path.

She shook her head and spoke in a quiet voice, "Should you be out here, so soon after?"

"Positive, I can talk to you, that's huge for me."

Charlie asked Lori to meet him at the path to run, a week and a day after the accident.

They began with a walk.

"I didn't attend Angie's memorial, what about you?"

"I went to mass, but not to the reception after. It's just so horrific, yeah, that's the word Lori, horrific.

"Have you heard about Carlo, in the trauma center in Atlanta?

"Latest, he's in an induced coma, swelling in his brain from the concussion. The question, when will he come out of the coma."

"His folks?"

"Coping."

"Jesse?"

"Back in school, quit cross country, charges pending. We talked about his lack of good judgement as he drives."

"And Angie?"

Charlie stopped walking and turned to Lori.

"Oh Lord," Charlie started to sob, then broke out crying.

Lori took him in her arms and let him cry. They stood together several minutes before Charlie settled down.

"She's with God, in heaven, don't you think?" Charlie asked as he stepped back away from her.

He watched her glittering green eyes gaze into his. Lori gave him her wide smile and nodded.

They continued their walk. Lori glanced over to him.

"He's calmer, good. And Lord, you know where Angie is now."

She swallowed hard at that thought.

Lori started jogging, picking up speed as she began to run. Winds whirled around her, enticing her to move along faster. After a while she heard him, his light stride behind her. Charlie passed her with a little wave of his good hand.

"He's getting better, it'll take a lot of time for him," Lori spoke out as she watched him in the distance ahead of her.

They just ran half the cross country route. She watched the slight limp of his right leg as they returned to the start of the run.

Sweat poured off their faces as they stood together.

"Charlie Garrault," she looked at him with tears mixing with the sweat, "God stood beside you, at the accident. It's His will you weren't injured worse. Do you understand how fortunate you were?"

She stopped talking and wiped her face.

"Charlie, students inches from you, one died and one may, or face unbelievable difficulties the rest of his life."

"Oh Lori, it's sinking into my pea brain. I got survivor's guilt, why did God spare me, and take another runner?"

"Dunno."

"He's got somethin' special He wants me to do."

Lori put her arm around his left shoulder as they walked.

"You may not know what that special thing is."

"Yeah."

"What now, we gotta go on livin', learn, get homework done, make grades. Somehow we gotta bring back some happiness in our lives. That's hard, with all that's going on, Charlie. Looking ahead, there's college, do something with that degree we strive for. Hey, maybe not oodles of money, but help out."

She let go of his shoulder and held his good hand. They walked to their cars. They hugged. Lori watched Charlie ease into his car.

"I got a lot to learn," he started to smile to her.

He showed her how hard it was to move his right arm out of the way so his left hand could change gears, from park to reverse.

"You're lucky you got an automatic."

℁

School and cross country moved along through November for Lori.

She received her official letter of admission from Georgia.

"Gotta tell you, we're still amazed. Lori, you done so good," Lars hugged his daughter and Nancy hugged her. She showed them her letter and information about the FAFSA the family filled out early in the fall. Lori's head filled with happiness for her future.

"My Board scores, they are what they are. I got admitted with my scores. Just know, Mom and Dad, that I'll need to work my rear end off to maintain the GPA the HOPE demands." She paused and nodded her head, "That is, if I get that scholarship."

Her parents watched her smile get bigger and bigger.

"You can do it, darlin', I know you can, " her dad nodded to her as they stood in the kitchen together. Nancy handed the letter back to her daughter. She looked from one set of eyes to the next.

"So much to celebrate this Thursday, Thanksgiving. Full-time for me, Dad's gettin' another raise, and Nils, he says he'll move out in January. He's found a place."

"Oh my gosh, I don't get to talk much to him. He's independent; it's great he's gettin' out on his own."

"He helped a bunch, with groceries, while mom recuperated."

"Dad, wow, that," she paused, "he's such a good guy."
She smiled to her folks.

"Nils, modest, we're a team, our family is."

Lori remembered last Thanksgiving. Her mom prepared more dishes than last year. She noticed that at the table as the family sat down.

Her dad kept the grace simple for the meal on that early Thanksgiving afternoon.

"I'd like to share something I learned in AP American History. In 1789 President George Washington made the first proclamation of Thanksgiving. I won't read through the whole proclamation, but he began by acknowledging the providence of Almighty God, to obey His will, to be grateful for His benefits, and humbly to implore His protection and favor.

That's how he began. He went on to share that both Houses of Congress, by joint committee, requested that he set aside a day of public thanksgiving and prayer."

"My goodness," Nancy smiled to her family, 'since 1789," she paused and shook her head, "that's a whole lot of years. Thank you, Lori, for letting us know about the day. I don't remember that President Washington did this, a very special day for our country."

They ate in the quiet of that afternoon. Everyone took second helpings. Lori noticed the family beginning to chat a little more. She thought through her thanks, for her family, for Bree, for her cross country team, including Charlie and her friend, Gavin. Tears came, sliding down her cheeks.

"You OK?"

"Got goosebumps now, still weep at times, thinkin' of Angie, and Carlo."

She gave her parents and Nils eye contact, "I'm blessed, thank you Mom, Dad, and Nils."

℘

Lori ran in the cross country team's last four-school meet out of town. On that November afternoon she came in second in the women's division.

"It's OK, I know I can run with the wind."

She whispered through her labored breathing as she went from running to a slow jog. She stopped, putting her hands on her hips and lowering her head.

"I gave it all I had, this was for you guys who're not with us, Charlie, Angie, Carlo, and Jesse."

Lori paused, her mind racing, "And I noticed Charlie as I ran. He came to cheer us on, thanks Charlie," she spoke out.

She lifted her head, smiling, "Be happy, Lori, your body, your mind, so lucky to have these abilities."

"Before you get off the bus, I want to talk to you."

Coach stood near the bus driver after the ride home.

"Team, I'm very proud of your efforts, all season long."

He shook his head, taking off his cap. Everyone watched him begin to cry.

"Unbelievable," Coach shook his head, "what happened to our team. Yet we kept on going, kept attending meets when I suspect you didn't even want to run."

He paused, "You did it for the four missing teammates. Believe me when I say, your constant courage showed me the depth of character each of you has.

You will continue your striving in your school work, and on into college. I've talked to all of you. All my seniors plan to further their educations past high school. I've learned one thing," he waved to the group, "everyone of you will persevere, in your own way. It's my privilege to spend time with you. I look forward to next season with my younger team members. I hope you all will return next fall."

Lori watched him give eye contact to each and every team member as he spoke. When he eyed her she saw tears and the strain of the past weeks in his tired eyes.

 The team stood from their seats shouting out, "Hip Hip Hurray, Hip Hip Hurray, Go Coach."

They clapped and cheered as coach watched them walk off the bus. Many of the team members hugged him.

When Lori got to him she hugged him.

She whispered, "Thanks Coach, for everything. It's been a once in my life-time experience."

She stepped back, giving him her widest smile. He smiled and nodded to her.

࿔

Lori planned out her studying for finals the week before Christmas. She looked forward to late afternoon runs after she accomplished those finals. Charlie caught up with her in the parking lot the day before the holiday vacation. He broke into a smile as they stood together.

"Wishing you and your family Happy Holidays, are you all staying here?"

She nodded and wished him Happy Holidays.

"Your arm?"

His smile disappeared as he shook his head, "It's not healing up as fast as I'd like, but the doc says the X-ray looks good. Maybe I'll get the cast off in a couple of weeks. Sophia's coming home. Dad's coming over for Christmas dinner; Mom invited him. He's got his own place; I slept over once."

They walked to her car. He hung his head down and shook it.

When he lifted it she saw his tears.

"It's awful, awful hard."

She heard his voice crack and moved closer to him.

"I pray for you, and for all your family."

Her gut cramped as she looked into his eyes. They hugged for a long time.

"George's?"

"Uh huh, my first late afternoon there, finals done."

"Take care."

"Happy Holidays, Charlie."

&

Bree called her.

"Merry Christmas, oh gosh."

"Long time," Lori completed the phrase.

"I been prayin', since I got your news about your team, the losses. I'm prayin' for you, that your sadness will one day be gladness, like for the birth of Baby Jesus."

"Thanks Bree, your semester?"

"Hard, Lori, takin' calc, AP stuff. I tried out for high school choir. That's fun."

"Like I enjoyed cross country. So great to wrap your mind around a different skill. I sure know you've got a voice. Admitted?"

"U. of New Mexico, boards excellent. I'm excited. Helping dad, secretarial stuff mom used to do. She likes working full-time for the city."

"Your emotions, Bree?"

"God's with me. It'll be a glorious Christmas. Grandmee's coming and dad's gonna stay on a third year. His church administration gave consent. So proud of him, the little church grows. A project the church put off is really happening, thanks to an anonymous donor."

"One year, what a difference."

"Oh my gosh, Lori, that's for sure. My crazy mind got pulled apart in many ways last Christmas. Scary, not knowing what went on with my body. It got better when I started at the school spring semester. We all faced pregnancy, school, homework. And we prepared for going on with the rest of our lives."

"Can't wait to see Gavin, since way last summer. Full time at George's right after Christmas, until classes start. Then I work Saturdays and three afternoons a week after school. I plan to stay on until August. UGA, I'm excited, scared, happy."

"Some happiness's coming back, Lori. So long since I've know what that's like. It's kinda like a warm soft light surrounding me. I started a little choir at church. We performed during Advent and from now on. A church member plays the piano. I lead the group and sing alto. For Christmas we'll sing a song in Spanish. Our church, pretty much bilingual."

"Do you sing "Mary's Boy Child?""

"Yes, the more I do, with church, and at school, gosh, it makes me excited for each new day. That's been missing in my life. Just surviving each day to go on to the next day, it's so over for me."

"That makes me happy, Bree, to hear you talk like that. It's the best Christmas present I could ever get from you."

Bree heard the lilt in her voice.

"Good luck this next semester, Lori."

"Same to you, Bree, I love you."

"I love you, Lori, Happy Christmas."

ℰℭ

"My last Christmas, at home."

He watched the light shining in her eyes.

"So surreal, lookin' back at all my other Christmases," she shared with Gavin. She took his order as he sat at the counter at George's.

"I want to see you, Lori."

"What about tomorrow, my house, some delish Black Forest cake needs eating, left over from Christmas dinner."

She paused, taking in his smile, including his dimples.

"Uh huh, saved back cake 'cause I wanted you to visit me."

"Ooohhh, bribery with food, of course I'm coming, conversation and cake, 7:30?"

"Perfect," she gave him her wide smile.

He noticed her eyes, now shiny and warm, "She's doing good, I can tell."

Gavin heard pleasant conversation all around him in this cozy café. All through his tasty meal of hamburger and fries he kept an eye on Lori. She worked in smooth, precise motions, whether it involved handling a tray of food, or a single order like his.

He watched her smiles and her courteousness to her customers. The locals liked Lori. Gavin heard them asking her questions about her future. They spent time talking about the Georgia Bulldogs and the way their season finished. She slipped his bill near his coffee cup, poured him more coffee and nodded to him, smiling. He gave her a generous tip, knowing this would help her pay for college, through hard work waitressing for now.

Lori had the next day off. She helped Nils move after they spent the morning cleaning up the one-bedroom apartment.

"Eeekkksss," she shook her head to her brother, "my standards of clean are not those of whoever cleaned this place before your move in."

"Hey, all I know is that they said it got cleaned."

Lori stuck her head out of the bathroom. She rolled her eyes. Then she saw her bro smile. He strode past her wheeling the upright vacuum. He started in on the small living room. He saw the thumb up from her. They returned to their home and filled both Nils and her cars with donated items from their folks. Back they went to his apartment.

They unpacked and put items away. Lori looked around, then stepped into the bedroom.

"It's empty; what's the plan?"

"New mattress, delivered tomorrow."

"That's it?"

"Can't afford anything else; I'll be comfy with just the mattress on the floor."

Lori stood in the middle of the living room, hands on hips.

She gazed at her brother and nodded her head, "It'll be just right, when you get stuff arranged your way."

Lori hugged her brother and left for home. She fixed dinner and they ate. She wanted to be ready for Gavin coming over. Lori made fresh coffee and had cake on the table. She looked around the neat kitchen, dishes finished and put away after the meal.

She thought, "Thank you, Bree, unbelievable what a little effort each day can do for a room, or a home."

℃

Gavin arrived. They hugged. As they stepped away from each other he asked, "You're taller," he paused, "right?"

She smiled to him, nodding, "Yeah, an inch, I had a growth spurt last summer, the running, working, and really concentrating on standing up straight and tall."

They sat across from each other at the kitchen table

"Good coffee."

"My folks insist on that."

"Lori, cake's delicious, the cherries and chocolate, oh my."

"My favorite cake to make."

"Please, Lori, catch me up, last summer."

"Missed you," she paused and he saw tears forming in her eyes. "Worked, George's, school, hard, studied every chance I had. But the Rail Trail, accomplished so much. I got to know you."

Gavin watched her give him her wide smile, her eyes now smiling.

"I want to hike the trail before classes start again. Straight A's for this finished semester. I'm pretty sure I qualify for the HOPE. Plus FAFSA's done. I will qualify for financial aid, possibly the PELL."

"Yeah, my understanding, PELL doesn't have to be paid back. But that's only for certain majors where there's a serious need, like for teachers."

"That's also what I'm told. I gotta back up, Gavin, my SAT and ACT scores were not good."

She stopped and nodded, "I'm happy to be admitted to UGA. I just drifted along, in my little isolated world. An Admissions person at Georgia saw my improvement. Would you like more coffee?"

"Please."

He observed her quick motions, the same way she moved in a graceful way at George's.

"Yeah, heard about the cross country team. It's great you ran with the team. When did you find out you could run?"

She gave him eye contact, "Do you remember Sophia, from our trail team?"

"Yeah, so strong, fit, she handled the work, just like you."

"Sophia ran cross country. One weekend she asked me to go on a run with her. Hey, I found out I ran fast, no idea about that."

She smiled, "Found out every time I ran, I got a runner's high." She shook her head and her eyes widened, "Didn't feel my feet touching the ground."

"What an experience you had!" Gavin exclaimed.

"Yeah, and I waited on the cross country coach at George's. He introduced himself and told me he heard of me. He asked me to try out for the team. I did and I made the team. I had a wonderful time, loved the exhilaration of running."

She stopped talking and he saw her thin lips and shake of her head.

"I didn't work at George's fall semester, just ran cross country, the meets and practices. And the school work, all grinding, hard. I made no money."

"You found something you loved."

"Right."

Lori started to tear up. Gavin touched her shoulder as he sat across from her.

"Please go on, Lori."

She heard the kindness in his soft voice.

"Devastating, losing Angie. Carlo, don't know about his condition now. Did you know them?"

He shook his head to her, "Dad told me. Pray, I do, for all of you, the whole team. First time, I think, if memory serves me, that Ony Springs High lost a student in our era."

"The whole town, in despair, everyone is. Jesse, the driver, I hear he doesn't want to live. The tragedy of Angie."

Lori ran her hand over her forehead. Her eyes filled with tears, "Jesse dropped out of school. Didn't finish the semester. I've watched him running the school's cross country workout trail. Jail time, don't know."

He watched her shake her head, "Gavin, this tragedy, I ask God. He's not answering."

She let out a cry, "I got this horrible thought about Jesse. And for Lord's sake, we still don't know if Carlo's gonna make it."

"Uh, a fourth person?"

"Yeah, Charlie, his arm broken. I talked to him before Christmas. I don't know about him. None of us're in our right minds."

He saw her tears again.

"You know what I'm sayin'."

"I do, Lori."

Gavin nodded to her, his face solemn, "Did you try to celebrate Christmas?"

"Yes, they tried, mom and dad and Nils."

Lori put her head in her hands. Quiet held in the kitchen and throughout her home. Her folks rested in their bedroom.

"I dream about the accident, sleep poor. My minister and I chatted. Time, it'll take time, for all of us. What you can do is keep us in your prayers."

She raised her head, nodding to him.

"Working at the café, and studying, going to class, I believe, Lori, will save you. You'll be so busy maybe not a lot of time to dwell on the bad stuff."

She touched his shoulder, "Yes, that'll be best, prayers, and church. Some advised me to start at a community college, so much less expensive. But my major, they don't know what I want. At UGA I'll start in on major courses, courses I couldn't get at a cc."

"Lori, what's your plan?"

"I helped little kids at an elementary school for a semester. I loved my after-school time with the kids. My decision, I want to work with younger children as a teacher. But not the tiny ones, 4th through 8th grade, so could be elementary or middle school."

He watched her shining eyes, filled with light, "That's awesome, Lori, there's such a teacher shortage."

"Not a lot of money to start, but I'll keep taking classes, get a Masters. I will do it for my love and care of young people, my service to society."

She gave him her wide smile.

"Gavin?"

"Started in summer, best thing I ever did, some classes out of the way, in a shorter time. I still live in the dorm, like summer. Dorms, I think, got fixed up for '96 Summer Olympics. I hate cooking. Chow's good in the dorm."

He shook his head to her and blew out a breath.

"Classes very intense, kinda looks like I'm headed toward civil engineering. I'm liking the water part, bridges."

He stopped talking and took her hand resting on the table.

"Engineering, so many ways to go in that field."

She squeezed his hand, "Your grades?"

"Good, I work my butt off. Sleep, maybe four hours, midnight to four a.m. Then I get up and study again."

Lori let out a "WHEW," and crossed her eyes to him. They laughed together.

"Engineering students, group work in classes?"

"Right, we're a close group." He gazed at her and nodded. "We're like the team that created the rail trail. And group projects like you asked, in our first year classes. Profs understand we'll be in team situations when we get into the real world. I gotta do an internship, soon as possible, next summer. And then I'll do maybe two more after that. Internships'll help me see what's out there."

"Charlie, he's my friend. We ran cross country together."

"The guy, broken arm, in that horrible accident?"

"Uh huh, we talk, like me and you. He knows we're going in different directions in our lives. No sexual pressure, just a pleasant friendship."

Gavin chuckled. She saw a shine in his eyes.

"Not so many women at Tech. I lost my virginity, there are a couple of sweet things I like. But I wanted to tell you, Lori."

He watched her wrinkle her forehead.

"And?"

"And I get back here. You're young, innocent, refreshing. You just don't care about a lot of stuff females at Tech are so hung up about. The guy, the car to go with the guy, scoring the guy."

He stopped talking and gave her googly eyes.

"The competition, so it seems, between some of the women, don't get it. I thought I came to Tech for an education. The women, super bright, engineering types, but they got this deal about gettin' a guy."

Silence held for a minute.

He gazed into her warm green eyes, "Maybe I'm runnin' with the wrong crowd."

"I think not, Gavin," she looked him over as she thought college women might, "you are handsome, pleasant, have your head screwed on straight, have common sense. You're not alcoholic or a druggie."

She nodded her head three times, "I'd say, you are a mighty fine dude."

He gave her googly eyes as he shook his head, "Not what I expected to hear from you," he paused, "my dear."

"Oh, smart, very smart, you are," she gave him a deep nod.

"Lots going on, stuff to do, in Atlanta."

"I bet," she smiled

"I'm headed back; New Year's Eve a girl I'm seeing's asked me to a party in Alpharetta, her parents' home."

Lori shrugged her shoulders.

"That's a north suburb of Atlanta. I'm staying with her and her family (separate bedrooms)."

He gazed at her.

"Uh huh, I see your questioning eyes."

"So life's good; how's your dad?"

"Real good, he's seeing a lady."

"So glad for him, it's been?"

"Years, time for him to get back out there; he's got a lot of living yet to do."

He touched her shoulder, "Your eyes're gettin' tired. I can see the strain you've been under, with your not sleeping."

"Time," she paused, "got your hike in on the rail trail?"

"Yeah, spent time at the fairy path, talking to mom, you know that's my special place for me and her."

She smiled to him and nodded, "I remember you telling me that."

He helped her carry the dishes to the sink. She turned to him. He touched her cheek and smiled to her.

"I will always love you."

Lori patted her heart with her hand, "And me," she paused, "you."

They hugged and gave each other a soft kiss. She helped him with his coat.

"I'll see myself out; it's December cold."

She caught his eyes with hers, "Godspeed, Gavin."

He nodded.

"Those green pools of her eyes, unforgettable," he thought as he walked down her front porch.

She washed and dried their dishes and put them away. Lori sat in front of the bright lighted tree, a bigger one this year.

"Will I ever see him again?" she asked herself.

From her memory she pulled scenes of Gavin and her.

"A special friend, thank you Man upstairs, for my relationship with Gavin."

7

"Happy, so awesome, to be back on the trail," Lori spoke out to the leafless trees on the cloudy and misty morning. She approached the fairy garden path. She snapped the last two pictures on her roll of film. Lori stood, taking shots from two different angles. She wanted to get the roll of film developed the next day.

With small strides she walked along the fairy path. She picked upt twigs that fell in the past few windstorms.

"Oh Gavin," she watched his image appear near her. "Your mom, yeah, I know she knows, the carvings, they're holding up good."

His image faded as she stopped and patted the wizard's head. She stepped to the end of the path. Looking back, hot tears burned her eyes.

"I helped do this, an effort I'll never forget."

Lori moved up the trail with her long stride. She stopped at Log Landing and sipped water. She munched on her trail mix of nuts and dried cranberries.

"Yum, tummy you love this stuff," she murmured as she started down. She came upon two sets of hikers, little children and their parents. Lori stepped aside so they could move up the trail.

"Good morning," she greeted them and they replied. She saw their smiles.

"Wow, it makes me feel great; hikers use this trail. I hope the kids like the fairy path," she breathed out as she smiled.

She kept that smile and happy thoughts on the way back to the trailhead.

଼ଡ଼

"Wanta run the cross country path?"

"Hey, Happy New Year, Charlie, glad you called. Yeah, I wanta run. I'll be workin' at George's once school begins."

They hugged as they met at the start of the path. Lori stepped back and noticed.

"Hey, cast's off."

"Uh huh, got exercises to do. Arm's stiffened up a lot. Doc says it was time. Yeah, yeah, like you told me, I'm trying not to fall."

He smiled to her, "Did you get to see Sophia?"

"Right, we met for lunch. We talked about working the rail trail. That was a once in a lifetime experience for me. Change, I changed that summer; trail workers became my friends."

Charlie moved along at Lori's slower running pace.

"Talk?"

"Tell me."

"I'm in counseling; I think it's gonna help."

"Yeah?"

She turned her head to him.

He watched her smile.

"Uh huh, maybe I could invite you to go along with me sometime, 'cause I know you got sadness from the accident."

"Hey, a good idea, Charlie. I'm not sleeping much, seen my minister once. The accident, which I didn't even see, keeps coming to me in various versions, nightmares. In a lot of them, Carlo and Jesse also die. Have you heard how Carlo's doing?"

"Last I heard, he came out of the induced coma. He's still not talking or recognizing people and incidents yet. Rehap hospital, I think that's next, to regain his abilities."

"Oh, that's positive, what you say. I pray to God his mental abilities, he took a massive hit to his head."

"I'm being positive. Carlo planned on college, not sure where."

Lori picked up the pace, as she thought, "Keep your mouth shut, in one nightmare Charlie dies."

"I'm gonna let you fly by, Charlie. I know you got soccer going on real soon. Meet back at the start of the path?"

"Yup, I'll do my exercises to prep for soccer 'til you get back."

Charlie circled around and around in her mind for the rest of her run.

She spoke out, "I'm encouraged, for Charlie." She shook her head as she passed by rustling tree after tree on the running path. "He didn't say a word about school, his plans for next year. It might be too soon. Maybe he needs to take it one day at a time."

She stopped speaking out and slowed her pace as she saw Charlie near their cars.

"Very cool that you ran with me, Lori. I always feel more upbeat when I talk to you." He smiled to her, noting her lustrous green eyes, "You are my special friend counselor."

"Like Bree was to me," she nodded to him.

"It's gonna be a crazy fall semester, school and work for you, for me school and soccer."

She spoke in a choking voice, "Our last school year, Charlie."

Lori watched as Charlie teared up, "I'll, I'll be relieved, for it to be over."

"Each day's precious."

"Very precious."

They hugged and walked hand in hand to their cars. Heading home, Lori thought ahead, "Cook dinner for my family. Nils might stay for a game after dinner. But my folks must get to bed, always work for them."

℘

"Mom, I'm doing good in school, and this last semester, fun in a couple of my classes."

They fixed dinner together that evening in late January.

"I'm so glad, Lori. Finding learning to be fun, oh how wonderful . You attend a fine little high school. For sure, our teachers and staff take care of our young people. Working

Saturdays and three afternoons a week, is that going OK for you?"

"It feels good to be making money, Mom. That's the one thing that really bothered me, during the fall. I loved cross country, but I got a lot of catching up to do, money-wise."

Nancy came from the stove and gave her daughter a hug. They stepped away from each other.

"Hey, pretty wonderful to discover a skill you didn't realize you had, right?"

Lori nodded to her mom, "The past three years, they've been years of discovery, as you say."

"And your helping around our home, I cannot say enough about how I like our home, bright and clean. That's because of you and your sweet friend, Bree. I come home to calm."

Lori watched as her mom's eyes teared up.

"I, I'm missing you, even though it's months before you leave for Georgia."

"You and dad, what's the name, empty-nesters, with Nils out on his own."

"For sure, it'll take getting used to," her mom came to her with another hug.

&

"Please Lori, I need your help."

She heard the tension in his voice, almost a cry.

"What's up?"

"Jesse called me just now. He's having a tough day. He wants me to come over. I, I do that about once a week."

Lori started to sweat as she continued to listen to him.

"Uh, he needs to talk to somebody besides me, someone not in the accident."

"Of course, maybe I c'n offer encouragement. He'll be leaving for a time."

"That's coming up soon. Do you need his address?"

"No, I'll see you soon. I just got home from school. You didn't have soccer?"

"No practice today."

Lori saw Charlie's car parked in front when she got to Jesse's an hour later. No one came to the door after she rang the doorbell several different times. She felt the doorknob turn in her hand.

"Not locked," she hollered out, "Jesse, Charlie, you guys, hey anybody home?"

She heard no sound. She walked into the living room and turned, noticing clouds gathering as she looked out the window. Lori continued into the kitchen and saw a coat on the floor by the doorway into the formal dining room. She moved past the coat and looked into the room.

"Jesse, Charlie," she gasped.

Lori turned around and took two steps. She collapsed in front of the dishwasher.

A white light burned her eyes as she looked ahead. A warmth spread around her. She heard a whisper, "911, Lori."

The warmth moved with her as she stood up. She searched the kitchen for a phone.

"It's on the wall, pick it up," she commanded herself. After she made the call she repeated the Lord's Prayer, over and over again. She eased herself to the floor, nauseous, tears flowing.

After a time she heard sirens, "Thank you, Lord," she croaked out.

"Lori?"

A male voice shouted out to her. Then other voices joined his.

"Kitchen."

The warmth decreased around her.

"Let me help you up, Lori."

The uniformed officer led her from the floor to the kitchen table and asked her to sit in a chair. He stayed with her and held her hand.

Tears blazed in her eyes as she looked into the eyes of the brown-eyed officer.

She squeezed his hand, "Thank you for staying with me, I'm in shock. I only looked into the formal dining room for several moments. Now I can smell it. Charlie, is he, is he gone?"

"Don't know that, Lori. We'll find out. Thanks to you we have your names. We're calling your parents. Your folks will come. I'll need your statement."

"Uh huh, you gotta have the facts."

Lori's mind jumbled through the information as she gave it to the officer. He stayed with her the whole time. She also heard low voices coming from the formal dining room.

"Please come with me, Lori," the officer requested. "We'll sit in the cruiser and wait for your folks."

The officer sat in the front with Lori in the back seat. She heard the radio, with its bleeps and blips. Two ambulances and police cars with flashing lights appeared. Several unmarked vehicles pulled up around the house. Lori noticed yellow police tape surrounding the front yard.

She eyes widened and she breathed fast, "Sir, sir, that's my dad coming toward us."

"Please stay in the car. I need to talk to your dad."

She observed her dad gesturing and shaking his head toward the officer as they talked. In a few minutes the officer appeared and let her out of the cruiser. Lori stood, looking up at her dad.

"Dear Lord, help her, my daughter," Lars thought as he took Lori in his arms. They held on to each other for a long time.

"Lori, we must leave."

They separated and Lori whispered to him, "Dad, I'll meet you in the ER."

She watched his forehead wrinkle and his eyes widen, "Lori, are you OK to drive?"

He saw her nod. He decided not to argue with her. Her ghost-white skin and bright eyes caused him to tremble.

They spoke in the ER, " Charlie, if he's still with us, he'll be here, Dad."

After Lars conversed with the ER staff, Lori talked with a nurse practitioner. She gave Lori medication to help her sleep along with a prescription to help her in the future.

The NP stepped away from Lori and took Lars aside.

"Her sleeping problems, since the accident, were you aware?"

Lars shook his head, "She's silent, so close-mouthed. Our minister talks with her."

"What she observed today, it'll exacerbate that accident situation."

"Lori'll return to her routine, I'm confident. She's a very busy kid, school, she works, and graduation's coming."

The NP smiled to Lars and nodded, "That's all good. Lori asked about Charlie. I'm finding out now. I'll release her. She insists she stays in the ER waiting room, until she knows about him."

Nancy joined Lars and Lori in the ER waiting room. 15 minutes later the NP returned.

"Lori, he's here with us. The doctors are keeping him."

"The Lord watches over us all." Lori smiled to the NP, "Yeah he needs to be here. He needs a complete psych eval. He and I, we even talked about that, after the accident last fall."

"You guys, friends?"

"Uh huh, we run together, buddies. And we are on the school cross country team."

Her parents saw her wide smile, seeing her happier face in that instant.

Lori slept dreamless, for the first time since the November accident. She jerked awake at 5 a.m., hustling to the kitchen to turn on the coffee. She returned to the floor by her bed, looking over her books, set aside just so last night. She got her coffee and dug into her homework.

"God, You're in charge, please help Charlie," she whispered. She said a prayer and returned to her studying.

∞

After work at George's the next evening, Lori's mom mentioned a message from Charlie. She listened to it.

"Got your message, Charlie, the hospital?"

"So noisy, hard to rest, I gotta see you."

"When're you comin' home?"

"Tomorrow, many counseling sessions, plus so much homework. A friend's picked it up and it'll be waiting for me when I get home."

"I'll drop by after school, just a few minutes 'cause of homework, not a work afternoon, but I gotta make dinner for my family."

"Thank you Lori, lots of explaining for you."

Lori chilled up as she walked to Charlie's front door. Her tummy cramped; she tasted vomit.

They hugged. He wore a sweater, but Lori could see the very edge of bandages as they walked along.

"Want a pop, at the kitchen table?"

She nodded. They sat across from each other and drank their pop. Charlie watched Lori as her face heated to a bright red. Her green eyes picked up a brightness he did not see before.

"Talk to me, you look like you're ready to explode."

"What's going on, Charlie?" she whispered.

"I show up. I see Jesse with his face all blood. You're on the floor in a pool of blood. I stood in the dining room for a couple of seconds. Seemed clear to me that I saw a double suicide."

"Wrong, you ready to listen?"

Lori nodded, hissing "I'm angry, so angry, Charlie."

"I know."

She watched him blow out a deep breath.

"I called you after Jesse called me. His front door stood open a little. I rang the doorbell. No reply so I walked in and hollered, 'Jesse.' I walked to the kitchen, looked around. Then I smelled it, combination of gunshot and blood.

Like you saw Jesse sat in a chair in the formal dining room. I moved toward him and read his note on the table."

Charlie nodded to Lori, "Suicide. I went crazy, crying, sobbing, not thinking. I grabbed a butcher knife from the block of knives on the kitchen counter."

Charlie stopped talking. Lori watched the misery in his eyes.

"I kept saying to him, Jesse, I wanta be with you. Life's just not worth it. So much sadness, can't concentrate, gonna screw up my college plans. Let me just be with you, wherever you are."

Charlie shook his head. She heard his cries.

"Then?"

"I stood next to his chair. I put the knife to my carotid artery. I started to slice into the carotid. Something caught me, don't know what. I moved the knife and sliced into my wrists. I lay down on the floor next to Jesse. I remember saying, 'Jesse, I'm following along, don't wait for me."

They sat in silence.

He looked into Lori's eyes, "Getting here, calling 911, I owe my life to you."

She nodded to him, "You're already getting help, right?"

"I am."

Lori's eyes burned. She put her forehead down on the table. She took in a breath, let air out through her mouth. Five times she did that. Her panic subsided.

In slow motion she raised her head and looked at Charlie.

"I'm so sorry for what you ended up seeing. I thought you and me, that we could just talk to Jesse. What happened, Lori, a death of despair, lowest of human emotions."

She stared at him, "And then, what you did?"

"Insane, no doubt, docs got me on medication. God doesn't want me to try that again. Me, I always thought suicide, well, a gutless, cowardly thing to do."

She touched his hand, resting on the table.

"Uh huh, for certain."

"Gonna try to return to soccer, to my regular routine."

"That's what I'm doing, Charlie, back to what's supposed to be normal. I'll continue to go to counseling with my minister. I'm on meds for a little while, to help me sleep at night. It's helping."

"I'm glad, Lori, your friendship, it means so much to me."

She tried to smile to him, but here face stiffened, "I know."

She got up and took her glass to the sink.

"We gotta go on," she heard her voice croaking.

She looked away from him, grabbing her coat and putting it on after she got outside.

"Watch over me, Lord, watch over Charlie," she prayed.

Tears filled her eyes as she drove away. Her tears stopped as she walked up to her front porch. She sat on the floor, doing homework in her bedroom. She took a break to make dinner for the family.

On Saturday Lori started to come out of the fog of sadness that engulfed her since Jesse's death. She concentrated on customer service for the folks at her station. A big group came in about the time her shift got over.

"I'll head home after I service this group."

George nodded to her, smiling, "Thank you Lori, I count on you."

On the way home from the café she spoke out, "Indispensable at the café, yeah, help out at home as much as I can. Straight A's in my classes, best thing for me is to stay very busy. That's my promise to me."

જી

Lori kept that promise to herself through February, March and April. She hiked the rail trail on Sunday afternoons, twice a month. She talked to Gavin and his mom as she walked along the fairy path that April afternoon.

"I'm thinkin' of you both, hope Tech is good. Rachel, see how well all your carvings hold up, rain and wind, no damage so far. There's a boy, not seeing him, he's got big problems. I'm no counselor. It's hard to let go; I gotta take care of myself. That's what our minister tells me."

The rain started as Lori drove home from the trail. She decided to go to prom by herself. Other kids socialized, maybe danced a little. She took in a deep breath at that decision. At home she found the dress she wore last year with Gavin. She lay it on her bed and touched the soft blue fabric.

"Thank you Betty, for my dress. I'll wear it."

Her mom passed her room and heard her speak. She turned around and came back. Nancy peeked in.

"Sorry, I overheard, help you?"

She came to her mom, "Thanks, but I'll be OK. I got my eye on the prize, UGA, a degree."

Nancy watched her daughter's eyes light up, a luminous green.

"Nuthin'll keep me from that dream, that goal. That's why I work so much, it's for my future."

"Sounds great, Lori. I know all will work out for you."

Lori and her mom hugged. After her mom left, Lori held the dress to her body. She danced a tiny waltz step around and around in her small bedroom.

℘

Two Friday mornings before prom Charlie stopped at her locker. They exchanged hellos since she saw him last.

"Please come to prom with me, Lori."

She stepped away from him. He displayed his bright smile.

"I plan to meet a group at prom." She shook her head to him, "I don't know, Charlie."

"Let me know Monday; it's been too long, my running buddy."

Lori started to smile when she heard running buddy. Some caution in her head let go of the smile. She headed off to her first period class.

All through the weekend she kept his request in her head. Sunday afternoon she ran the cross country path, stretching out before she began. She picked up her pace, soon floating along. She made a decision.

Charlie caught her on her way to first period.

"Yes, thanks Charlie," she gave him a tiny smile, "I'll go to prom with you."

"Details later?"

She nodded, giving him a wave.

That night she danced tiny steps to the waltz, around and around her bedroom. She visualized his handsome presence in front of her. She fell into a dreamless sleep.

"Mom, Charlie asked me to prom."

Nancy touched her daughter's shoulder.

"It's been a distressing time for Charlie. Lori, you're serious, solid-minded. I suspect he is used to beautiful, but possibly shallow young ladies who are always among his classmates. I remember those young ladies from my own school days."

"I'm off at 3 p.m. that Saturday. George knows I have prom, but no circumstances."

Nancy smiled to Lori, "George, he really likes you. You're such a conscientious employee. You'll be a great help this summer. Dad and I plan some time off. It'll be nice for you to cover for me."

"Good for you to take some time off. I've never met a couple who work as hard as you two do."

Charlie left a voice mail for Lori on the Wednesday before prom. He couldn't go with her. A girl he'd been seeing gave him problems. Lori picked up her backpack and moved to her room.

"Dear Lord," she spoke out, "it was a dream, but one that wasn't meant to be. I'm so disappointed."

Lori got down on her knees and put her head on her bed. She cried, for all the sadness of the accident, of losing Angie, then Jesse. Charlie could'a died. And Carlo, now with a mental age of 12, learning to read, write, walk and talk all over again.

"God," she raised her head. "Change, so much ahead for me. Disappointment, that will continue to happen. I'll lose HOPE at UGA, if I don't make grades." She pondered for a couple of minutes. "And losing HOPE, I can't financially keep attending school. So I gotta move forward. I know You're right beside me, now, and tomorrow."

Lori wiped her tears away and blew her nose. She arranged her homework and began. She shifted to her housework chores for the day and made dinner. Tonight she'd just have her dad. Her mom worked a double shift for the day and evening.

ഔ

Lori swirled and twirled in a fast dance with a member of her cross country team. Her eyes caught the gold and silver crepe paper and flowers on the pillars all around the room.

"You look lovely tonight," Jason smiled to her as they moved around the floor.

"And you, dude, pretty fast on your feet!" Lori exclaimed as she looked up into his eyes.

"Still runnin', Lori?"

"Yes, try to get to the cross country trail twice a month, on Sunday afternoons. Saturdays I work at George's, also three afternoons after school. So not much time for runnin'."

"You do plenty of that at the café."

"Right, are you excited for graduation?"

He nodded down to her, "Yes."

"I'll be at Notre Dame."

"Yeah, Charlie also."

"I know," he nodded to her

"Take care, Lori, that was fun."

Jason escorted her back to her group.

"Thanks Jason," she smiled up to him.

"May I have this dance?"

Lori turned to the voice, Charlie's.

She looked into his eyes and nodded.

He held her close, smelling the light flowery perfume in her hair.

"You're beautiful, Lori. I'm so glad I've had a chance to get to know you. You are rock solid."

She pushed away from him for a moment.

He watched her green eyes brighten.

"You disappointed me, Charlie. No explanation, just know I can't count on you."

She shook her head to him, moving back closer to him.

"I know, Lori."

She watched tears form in his eyes.

"I'm sorry."

"Notre Dame, in your plans?"

"Gotta make great grades. Oh, my gosh, a horrible start to the semester, my idiot actions. Grades're better now. And my stupidity, drove my parents further away from each other. I caused them so much trouble. Dad isn't speaking to me right now."

"What's ahead of us, pretty scary, exciting, leaving home, starting on our new journeys."

"Oh Lori, I gotta start thinking about it that way. I'm on a new journey."

They held hands as he took her back to her table. Lori put her hand on Charlie's cheek.

"We'll have so much to learn, and have fun, too."

They smiled to each other and hugged.

℃

"I've done it."

She shivered as she gazed at the other graduates. She stood up with everyone else in the graduating class. Lori looked up into the pale blue sky watching puffy white clouds dance around.

"Thank you for my life."

Her senior class requested that the ceremony take place on the football field, a change from the indoor ceremony. They all wore black robes, not school colors with the guys in one color and the girls in another. Her parents and Nils found her as the graduates dispersed. She watched Charlie and Sophia approach. Charlie hugged her, and then Sophia gave her a hug. Everyone exchanged congratulations.

"Thank you for coming, Sophia."

Sophia smiled to Lori, "Had to watch my bro graduate and see you, too." She looked at him and held his shoulder, "Charlie's worked hard."

Her folks and Nils headed back to their jobs. Nancy planned a picnic in the back yard that evening to celebrate Lori's graduation and attending UGA.

Gavin called that afternoon to congratulate her.

"I'll plan to come to see you at UGA, I promise."

"Will look forward to that. Summer school for you?"
"Of course, and an internship, gotta have that."

&

"Graduated?"
"This morning
"And you?"
"Yesterday."
"No time to talk, all semester, Bree. Tell me."
"Hard semester, made great grades. It'll be UNM, excited."
"Your choir, who'll take over?"
"Training a singer. Great thing, our piano player's staying. That means the choir'll be here. My folks'll be here a third year."
"Where to for them next?"
"Stay in the states, uuummm, not sure."
"Hard semester for me, did grandmee tell you what happened with Jesse and Charlie?"
"She did, gosh, thought so much about you and prayed for you. Lori, seein' that, are you working with your minister?"
"I am, it helps. Lot of time at George's, will be full time this summer. I'll make all the money I can. Will be work study at UGA."
"Prom?"
"Met a group at the dance. A fun time, I had a date; he cancelled.
"Terrible."
"It was. I got a whole huge bunch of disappointments I'm gonna have to cope with. This is just the start."
"That's right, Lori."
"Prom for you?"
"Had a date and we had a good time. He'll attend UNM, too. He wants to be a medical doctor, real driven guy. Uh, me, I'm not sure."
"I predict social work, Bree, you been doing that all your life."

"Mmm, you might be right, but I got time to decide."

"I know where I'm headed."

"Yeah, little kids, that's awesome, Lori."

"I love you, Bree. You are my forever friend; you helped me become what I am today."

"I love you, Lori. You are my forever friend. We are always in His hands."

&

Lori enjoyed her summer at home before college. She remained positive and upbeat as she waitressed, sometimes more than 40 hours a week. Her days off varied. She filled in when other staff at George's took their summer breaks. At home she fixed dinners for her parents, with Nils joining about once a week. Some nights it was just her dad and her, with her mom pulling double shifts at the cafe.

She tended her small rose garden in the back yard and managed the yard and home. In the evenings she read books her favorite librarian, Margie, recommended. Looking at magazines in the library for ideas helped her to buy outfits for school. Working at George's meant Lori wore a waitress uniform. She also wanted a specific look to her appearance and clothes for college. She planned to use these outfits later as a teacher.

"I always want to look professional," she shared with her mom. Together they went through her outfits after she bought them all. Some she tried on for her mom. Nancy expressed her opinion.

"Thanks, I'm glad you think my clothes are OK, " she smiled to her mom. Her look included: three pairs of slacks, tops to match, three winter plaid skirts, three other skirts for spring and fall, three turtle necks and an all weather jacket for both rain and cold. And she had shorts and a t-shirt for her dorm kitchen duty. She liked tights so got six pairs for all her outfits. She envisioned herself as a teacher with a pleasant, casual appearance.

"I'm getting so excited," she confided with Bree as they called each other. "And I'm scared. Can I cut it?"

Bree's reply remained, "Of course you will do good. You are motivated and such a hard worker."

The teens shared their worries and hopes. Bree saw her campus for the first time that summer.

"I wanta be at UNM so bad, Lori. I'm sorry you couldn't go to visit UGA this summer."

"It just didn't work out, George's the issue with employees taking summer time off. And I'll be gone from there soon. But hey, I've already memorized the map of the campus so I'll get around easy when I arrive."

They said their goodbyes to each other.

"You are in my thoughts and prayers, Bree."

"As you are in mine, Lori."

&

Lori's summer passed like a fast moving storm. Nils rode along with Lori's parents as they made their way from north Georgia to Athens and her dorm.

"I gotta pinch myself, so excited to move on with my life," she shared with Nils as their car drove through the maze of cars, students, and parents headed for a particular dorm. When they arrived at Lori's room, the space filled with another family. Lori found her way to the tall auburn-haired teen.

"I'm Lori Grifson."

They shook hands as Cami introduced herself.

"I'm Cami Eversen."

She introduced her parents, Sam and Dena, and her twin brother, David.

Lori introduced Nancy, Lars, and Nils to them.

"What a basketball team we'd have," Dena giggled as she gazed around the small space at the tall people in the room.

They all laughed and agreed.

"We need to leave," Sam smiled to them all, "have to get David back to Georgia Tech. We all helped him move in to his dorm last week."

"But I had to be here to make sure Cami is all set for her college adventure."

"Yeah, everybody, David and I've always been close."

"Right, ever since she arrived 3 minutes after me."

Dena added, "A wild and crazy time for Sam and me."

"Expected," Nancy asked, "twins?"

Dena and Sam laughed, "Not until a couple of months before."

"Oh my gosh!" Lori exclaimed.

Everyone joined in with laughter.

"We'll leave for a bit and let you say your goodbyes," Lars spoke out.

The Grifson's returned to their car. Nils heaved her clothes over his shoulder, all set up on hangers. Nancy and Lori each carried a suitcase filled with Lori's stuff. Lars managed the bedspread and sheets Lori wanted for her bed. The laptop computer, Lori's prized possession, she carried that in its carry case with her other hand. And she wore her backpack full of underwear. Nancy carried the bag with Lori's shoes. Lori directed the placement of her suitcases and bag of shoes under her high rise bed. Nils hung her clothes in the closet as she placed her laptop and equipment on her desk.

"I've brought just the amount of stuff I'll need. My space is about the size of my room at home…nice."

She turned to her parents and Nils. Tears held in her eyes as she hugged each of them.

"I love you all," she whispered.

Now she watched tears coming from all three sets of eyes. They departed for the long drive back to Ony Springs.

Lori stood at the dorm window gazing out at the blaze of trees, maples and oaks. She opened the window a fraction, hearing the sounds of the rustling trees.

"It's me, now, on my own, my time is mine, no more George's or the home or yard. School, each moment is precious, Lori, have fun and be mindful of why you are here," she spoke out. "YOU are in charge and I will follow the plan YOU"VE set for me." She added, "As best as I can."

ହଠ

"I'm El Ed, really little kids, pre-K and K," Cami shared with Lori.

"And I'm El Ed, 4th-5th graders."

"Teachers is what we'll be."

They smiled to each other at their common statement as they headed off to their first class of the semester.

Lori and Cami developed a friendship, almost from the beginning of their time rooming together. When Cami learned that Lori would not have a ride home for Thanksgiving because of her parents' complicated work schedules, she asked Lori to celebrate Thanksgiving with her family. Her brother planned to come home from Tech in Atlanta.

David wanted to get to know Lori better. He knew that from the moment he met her in Cami's dorm room. He saw her smile, but it was her shimmering green eyes that caught his attention. He shared his desire with his sister. An e-mail relationship sprouted between Lori and David.

The Eversen family lived in Monroe, about half way between Atlanta and Athens. Lori enjoyed her time with this funny warm family. Dena worked with middle school students in math. Sam practiced law with two other partners. They handled many city and county government issues, along with their particular interests, Sam's being family law.

David expressed zero interest in law. He built stuff, tinkered with engines, and liked his garden, corn, ethanol from corn his interest.

Lori saw the twins complementing each other, both tall, auburn-haired, with brown eyes. Cami smiled a lot; David took on a more serious look. And he reminded Lori of another boy.

"I'm glad we're at different schools," Cami mentioned that to Lori more than a few times. "I don't live in his shadow any more. His grades were better than mine, a scholarship for him at Tech, nada for me. But I love kids; he doesn't. So I enjoyed those years I babysat."

"I don't have experiences like that, Cami. I was a waitress, but did spend one year in an after-school experience with little kids at a school in my town. That's where I got excited about my future, kinda knew where I wanted to be."

Lori sensed the love in this family while she visited. She saw the caring in the eyes of Cami's parents for both their teens.

"These parents, and my parents, I see now about the feelings they have for us. We're lucky kids," she nodded her head as everyone prepared to leave.

Sam took Cami and Lori back to Athens. Dena drove David to Atlanta. Lori sent a thank you note to Cami's parents, using her favorite calligraphy. She wanted them to know how much she enjoyed her visit.

℘

She gazed around her tidy dorm room. Lori shut her door and walked through the windowed wing to the reception area. A flood of images filled her head: the first few weeks of classes keeping her slammed with homework. Having workstudy in her dorm kitchen forced her to manage her time. School started to make sense to her, an adventure she began to enjoy.

Lori stopped in the middle of the wing and gazed out at the brilliant reds and oranges of the trees shaking their leaves at her. She moved to the side, close to the window. She looked at her hands. They shook hard. She breathed in and blew breath out. After five times she saw the shaking lessen. She refocused as she entered the dorm reception area. Lori gazed around. Her eyes widened as she spotted him.

They walked toward each other.

"Those eyes," he paused, "she looks wonderful."

"He stands so straight and tall."

They hugged and held on.

"It's so good see you. Thank you for coming."

"I had to see how school is treating you."

They stepped away from each other and held each other's hands.

"Parking?"

"A few spots in the lot, guess 'cause it's Saturday."

"So super cool, for you to drive over to see the game with me here in Athens."

"It's an old rivalry."

"I see you're wearing your Georgia Tech sweatshirt, and I decided to wear my Georgia sweatshirt."

"I couldn't resist; it is a long-time rivalry."

He hugged her shoulder after they exited the dorm.

"Your semester?"

"Very technical, into our programs, so deep. You?"

"Favorite class is my first education course. It's like the history of education, how we got where we are today in educating our young folks. What surprises me is the cyclical nature of it all, like reading, for a while, phonics, like the sounds of words. And then there was a push for the whole word approach. At the moment it's a combination of those two practices."

"Hey, where are you taking us?"

"It's a pub, lots of TV's and of course the game will be on several of them."

They walked along, Gavin holding her hand.

"It feels good, natural," he turned to her as she turned to him, "holding your hand, hearing your voice, Lori."

She slowed her walking pace.

"Uh huh, same goodness for me. We got a friendship, holding strong through these past few years."

"About the reading you talked about, I so well remember writing stories, in first grade, didn't know much about the spellings. Lots of fun writing my tales. We read our stories to the whole class. I got lots of good chuckles from the other students."

"Aha, the funny guy," she smiled to him, squeezing his hand and gazing ahead.

They found a small table for two toward the back of the pub. Lori saw the supersize screen and heard the background noise of the crowd at the Georgia Dome. They watched the game, a rivalry between Georgia and Georgia Tech for many years. Yummy smells of cooking barbeque and hamburgers tickled their noses.

"Georgia's outclassing us, in every way," Gavin announced after they watched for a few minutes.

She gazed into his smokey gray eyes, "Wanted to thank you for the graduation card." She smiled, "Not expected, you are one thoughtful guy."

"Those luminous eyes, oh my," he thought. He caught her gaze, "Always got time for special people in my life."

"School's good for you," she nodded, "what about the little time you have to relax?"

"Well, I spend time with two very different women. One's super smart, the other one's got some common sense. The first young lady," he shook his head, "has absolutely zero in the common sense category."

They laughed together at his confession.

"My roommate's brother, we've met and we e-mail. He's at Tech."

His eyes riveted to hers, "You're still the hardest working young woman I've ever known. That summer creating the trail, my first real experience being around women in that close proximity, Sophia, yeah, the same way."

He nodded, "Guess I'm drawn to athletic women who know their own minds, like you. Except you're my one with the extraordinary eyes. Hey, what about cross country here?"

"No way, Gavin, that's too much of a time commitment. I work in my dorm dining hall, behind the scenes.   It's kinda like at George's. I help with food prep. I work breakfast and dinner, six days a week. The best thing is I eat for free. It really helps with room and board."

She raised her hands and clapped, "My grades, I'll keep the HOPE for next semester, with my good grades so far."

"Yeah, me too, I work hard. The HOPE is worth it. Great grades, a have- to, for finding that job I want."

They ordered food, for the part of the fourth quarter they wanted to see.

"Hamburger and fries, very good, how about for you?"

"Yes, very good."

They ate in silence as they watched the game finish. Gavin shared his disappointment with her.

"Tech only got 17 points, a bummer."

"Yeah, my Bulldogs pulled it off again with 34. They got a spectacular team."

"So glorious here, Lori, the maples and oaks in their bright colors. Your campus, so like how a college campus should look."

They held hands as they returned to her dorm.

"Thank you for the yummy food, Gavin."

She gazed up to him, smiling.

"You get a break in the morning, not having to serve."

"I have church. They have coffee and donuts after. That's my breakfast on Sunday."

"Please go on in to the dorm. I want a minute out here, one more look at the beauty."

Lori found a quiet corner in the reception area. She stood, waiting for him.

She whispered, "So many thoughts of you, Gavin, swirling about in my head. There'll be so many interesting students I'm gonna know as I experience college."

He found her, standing straight and tall, smiling to him. He moved close and touched her shoulder. They looked into each other's eyes.

"I love you, Lori."

"And I love you, Gavin."

They kissed, caressing each other's lips. They stayed in the kiss. Gavin and Lori stepped back from each other.

"Safe travels back to Atlanta. Good luck on finals. Oh, will you be home for Christmas? The holidays, coming soon."

He touched her arm, "Home, yes, dad has someone for me to meet. Good luck with finals and enjoy your break at home."

"Dad'll pick me on Saturday morning after finals. The dorm kitchen closes after breakfast."

Lori looked up into his eyes. He saw the luminous green, glazed with tears.

"So special, you're special to me," Lori patted her heart.

"Carry me on, Lori, in your thoughts."

They hugged, trembling.
She whispered to him, "As I carry you on, Gavin."

Baskets on Christmas Lane

19-year-old Jenny Grant witnesses a murder. She identifies both the killer and the dead person to federal authorities. Jenny Grant becomes Ann Farron. She is integrated into the Federal Witness Protection Program. Ann signs a contract to teach K-8 music and high school chorus. Music guides Ann in her journey to her new life. She meets Zach through her friend, Aunty Cal. Zach comes to practice law in Ony Springs after he is shot on the steps of a California courthouse.

Ann and Zach fall in love. Ann cannot ever reveal who she really is to Zach or anyone. They build their relationship together. After Zach's dad dies, he takes time away from seeing Ann. Ann struggles, knowing Zach is who she wants in her life. She moves on as she has to. With time Zach's grief loosens its hold. Ann and Zach renew their relationship and pledge to join their lives together.

Also available as an audiobook on Audible.

About Cathleen

www.CathleenEllis.com

Cathleen Ellis is a Colorado native. She and her husband, John, live in the northern part of the state. They have four sons, three daughters-in-law, and four grandchildren. Cathleen draws the inspiration for her love stories from the lives of young people with whom she has lived and worked her entire life.

www.ingramcontent.com/pod-product-compliance
Lightning Source LLC
Chambersburg PA
CBHW050147110726
47898CB00008B/2696